SECRETS IN DARK WATERS

CARLA CASSIDY

Harlequin

INTRIGUE

Harlequin® INTRIGUE™

ISBN-13: 978-1-335-69073-9

Secrets in Dark Waters

Copyright © 2026 by Carla Bracale

Recycling programs for this product may not exist in your area.

Harlequin Enterprises ULC
22 Adelaide St. West, 41st Floor
Toronto, Ontario M5H 4E3, Canada
www.Harlequin.com

HarperCollins Publishers
Macken House, 39/40 Mayor Street Upper,
Dublin 1, D01 C9W8, Ireland
www.HarperCollins.com

Printed in Lithuania

1 2 3 4 5 6 7 8 9 10 LIT 28 27 26 25

He stared at her for a long moment and then he grinned.

It was a transformative smile, softening the hard lines of his face and warming up the beautiful green of his eyes. It lasted only a moment and then fell away. "I have a feeling you can be quite a handful," he said.

"Trust me, I'll behave." Her own smile faded. "Thank you again, Jacque, and I'll see you day after tomorrow."

As Monique headed back to her cabin, a sweet anticipation swept through her. It was possible within a matter of days she would be able to name her mother's killer.

However, there was no question that she had a bit of apprehension in working with Jacque. She knew nothing about the man or what had originally brought him to the swamp. She was trusting the word of a stranger.

She just hoped she wasn't making a wrong decision in involving him. What she planned to do was already risky enough. She was on the hunt for a cold-blooded killer.

Carla Cassidy is an award-winning, *New York Times* bestselling author who has written over 170 books, including 150 for Harlequin. She has won the Centennial Award from Romance Writers of America. Most recently she won the 2019 Write Touch Readers' Award for her Harlequin Intrigue title *Desperate Strangers*. Carla believes the only thing better than curling up with a good book is sitting down at the computer with a good story to write.

Books by Carla Cassidy

Harlequin Intrigue

A Bayou Investigation

Murder in Dark Waters
Kidnapped in Dark Waters
Secrets in Dark Waters

Marsh Mysteries

Stalked Through the Mist
Swamp Shadows
Hunted in the Reeds

Harlequin Romantic Suspense

The Scarecrow Murders

Killer in the Heartland
Guarding a Forbidden Love
The Cowboy Next Door
Stalker in the Storm

Visit the Author Profile page at Harlequin.com.

CAST OF CHARACTERS

Monique Santori—In investigating her mother's murder, Monique finds herself in danger when the killer comes after her. Can she trust her new, handsome bodyguard?

Jacque LeBlanc—He is determined to keep Monique safe, but the last thing he wants is for his heart to get involved with her.

George Trahan—Is the man really a concerned neighbor or a killer looking for a way in?

Jackson Scott—Does the district attorney have justice on his mind, or is he really a cold-blooded murderer?

Pierre Guidry—Does the gator-hunter really have an alibi for Mystique Santori's murder or has somebody lied?

Louis Theriot—A fisherman who had been seeing the voodoo queen, Mystique. How desperate was he to make sure his secrets remained secret?

Chapter One

Monique Santori had a plan, albeit a potentially dangerous one. Since the murder of her mother almost four months ago, all she wanted was the killer behind bars.

Her mother, Mystique Santori, had been known as the voodoo queen in the swamp that half surrounded the small town of Dark Waters, Louisiana. People came to her under the cover of darkness to seek a charm or a spell to help them with a variety of problems.

She had been loved by some and feared by most as it was believed that she dabbled in black magic. Then one night somebody had come into her shanty and killed her by slashing her throat. At the same time Mystique's client book where she kept all her notes on her nightly visitors was stolen as well.

It had been four agonizing months for Monique and her two older sisters, who deeply mourned the mother they had lost. They had hoped for a quick arrest and justice for Mystique. Most people, including the law in Dark Waters, had believed that Pierre Guidry, a gator-hunter and Mystique's on-again-off-again lover, had been guilty of the crime. Unfortunately, they had no evidence to support arresting and charging Pierre. However, in the end, Pierre had an alibi for the time of the murder.

Still, the three sisters waited for an arrest to happen. However, Chief of Police Daniel LeCroix and his team didn't even have a potential suspect at the moment. The case had completely stalled.

But Monique was hoping to change that starting tonight. Since the murder, both of her sisters, Angelique and Dominique, had tried to find the killer and had instead found love.

Angelique had fallen in love with Daniel LeCroix and Dominique had found love with one of Daniel's detectives, Luke Madison.

Monique wasn't looking for love. She was looking for answers. She was definitely seeking a killer. As soon as she got off work today, she was going to put a plan into action to find the murderer who had stolen her mother from her. Even now, thoughts of her mother caused a swift shaft of grief to stab through her.

She looked at the wall clock in the store. She still had two hours to go before she would be off duty. Right now, she was the only person in the All That Jazz dress shop.

She got up from behind the cash register and walked over to the dress rack that held the items patrons had tried on that day but hadn't bought. She returned each article of clothing to the racks where they belonged and then went back to her chair behind the register.

At least she got off at four this afternoon and didn't have to work until close which was at nine. Normally, she didn't mind working long hours at the shop. She loved being a sales clerk and assistant manager.

But tonight she had other plans, so getting off at four would give her plenty of time. She would change her clothes, grab something to eat and then head out to find the man she hoped would help her.

A small shiver worked up her spine at thoughts of Jacque LeBlanc. She didn't know the man personally, but it was whispered that the mysterious gator-hunter knew about things that happened in the swamp. It was also rumored that he was an intelligent man, and she definitely needed a smart person in her corner.

The bell over the door tinkled, and Monique's oldest sister walked in. "Angelique, what a surprise," Monique said in greeting.

"Hi, sis." The two met in the middle of the shop and hugged. "How's business?" Angelique asked. She was clad in a pair of black slacks and a purple T-shirt with the logo of her store on the front. Mystique's Magic was an homage to the mother they had lost.

"It's been pretty slow today," Monique replied. "So are you here for a sisterly visit or are you here as a customer?"

"Both. I wanted to check in with you, but I also want to find something special to wear this evening."

"Why? What's happening this evening?" Monique asked curiously.

Angelique's light brown eyes glowed with barely suppressed excitement. "Daniel told me he was cooking me a nice, candlelit dinner tonight." She grabbed Monique's hand. "I think… I really think he's going to propose to me tonight."

"Oh, Angelique, I'm so very happy for you." She squeezed Angelique's hand and then released it. "And I know exactly what you're looking for." She led her sister to the loungewear rack where she pulled out a coral-colored two-piece. "This color will be gorgeous on you, and the scoop neckline offers just a little sexy tease. And best of all, it's twenty percent off that particular brand right now."

"Can I try it on?"

"Only if you let me see it on you," Monique said.

"Deal."

Monique carried it to the dressing room where she hung it on a hook and then stepped out and closed the door, giving Angelique privacy to change her clothes. It didn't take long for Angelique to step out wearing the new outfit.

"Oh, Angelique, it fits you perfectly," Monique exclaimed. "You look positively amazing in it."

Angelique studied her reflection in a floor-length mirror on the back of the dressing room door and smiled. "Sold," she said. "Just let me change back into my own clothes, and I'll be out to pay for it."

"Call me and tell me if he pops the question," Monique said a few minutes later as Angelique finished paying.

"You and Dominique will be the first to know," Angelique replied. "Oh, Monique, I'm so happy I could burst. Now if they would just arrest Mama's killer, then all would be right in my world."

The two visited for a few minutes longer, and after Angelique left the shop, once again Monique's thoughts went to her mission for the night. She knew both of her sisters considered her to be soft and fragile, but they didn't know the core of inner strength she had found since their mother's murder. She was determined to catch the killer.

She certainly wasn't going to share with her sisters

what she planned to do. They would try to talk her out of it. They would tell her she wasn't capable. As the baby of the family, she was often underestimated by her two older siblings.

However, it had been almost four months since the murder. She was no longer willing to sit on the sidelines and just wait for things to happen. It was time for her to act.

The rest of her work day went by agonizingly slowly as no other customers came in. At ten till four, Cynthia Orlick entered the shop. Cynthia was a bubbly young woman who was a new hire. Not only was she friendly, but so far she was always on time for her shifts and seemed to be very dependable.

"Hey, Monique," she greeted with a big smile. "How's business been today?"

"Slow…very slow," Monique replied.

"Then thank goodness I brought a book to read between customers," Cynthia replied. She stowed her purse under the counter as Monique pulled her purse out. "I know I'm a few minutes early, but you can go ahead and leave. I'll take it from here."

"Thanks, Cynthia. Hopefully you won't have too much of a boring night," Monique replied. The two said their goodbyes, and then Monique walked out into the stuffy August air.

The summer weather in Dark Waters, Louisiana, wasn't for the weak at heart. The little town sported hot temperatures and thick humidity. However, Monique didn't live in the town proper. She lived in the swamp that half surrounded Dark Waters.

It didn't take her long to drive from the store on Main

Street to the swamp's entrance where she parked her car among others.

The swamp begged her to enter its dark, mysterious depths. This was her home...where she had lived all her life. Alligators and wild boar, poisonous snakes and spiders as big as her fist also lived here. But as far as she was concerned, the beauty of the swamp far outweighed the dangers.

Tall cypress and tupelo trees rose up like sentinels, and Spanish moss dripped down like lacy icicles. Flowering bushes dotted the marshy landscape, and a variety of plants added an interesting visual element.

She entered the narrow path that would eventually take her to her shanty. Little animals scurried in the brush on either side of her, and the sun struggled to shine through the thick leaves overhead, making it cooler here than in town.

As she walked, once again she thought about her plan to catch a killer. It certainly wasn't too complicated. Still, she needed somebody to bounce her ideas off of. That was where hopefully Jacque LeBlanc would come in.

She couldn't talk to her sisters, who would throw a fit that she was involving herself in the investigation. She had no real close friends. Growing up, she'd always had her sisters as her best friends.

She reached her shanty and crossed a small bridge to the front door. The shanty where she'd grown up with her mother and sisters was deeper in the swamp and at the moment sat empty. Angelique had moved in with Daniel, and Dominique had moved in with Luke.

Monique was trying to decide if she wanted to move from her small shanty to the much bigger one. She loved her one-bedroom shanty which felt cozy, but there would also be a sweet familiarity if she moved into her childhood home. However, right now she had much more important things on her mind.

She went directly to her bedroom. The full-size bed was covered with a deep purple spread, and the single window sported matching curtains. A dresser was against one wall, and there were nightstands on either side of the bed.

She changed out of the long, forest green lacy skirt she'd worn for work and into a pair of jeans, exchanging her matching lace blouse for a more casual red one. She brushed out her long dark hair and then went into the small kitchen area to check the cooler.

Even though she had no real appetite, she knew she should probably eat something. She'd skipped lunch earlier and needed to eat before leaving to speak to Jacque.

Her muscles tightened as she thought of meeting with the virtual stranger.

She finally made herself a cheese sandwich, added a handful of chips and grabbed a soda, sitting at the table to eat. When she was finished, she turned off her phone and slid it into her back pocket. Grabbing her keys, she left the shanty.

It was early enough she hoped to find the gator-hunter at home; most of the men in his business went out in the late evening.

The deeper she went into the swamp, the cooler it got. Despite the comfortable temperature, she felt overly warm. Just her nerves. She told herself that the worst that could happen was he'd tell her he wasn't interested in brainstorming with her. But that thought didn't calm the nerves that jumped inside her.

She desperately needed somebody smart to talk to about her plans to get the evidence they needed to lock away a killer. That was the only way she could move forward in her life. As long as the murderer was out there walking free, she was stuck in the mire of her grief.

She passed a large pool of water where a gator swished its tail before disappearing from view. A red fox darted out, then scurried back into the brush for cover. It was as if all the animals around her felt her anxiety.

Jacque's shanty was tucked away in the middle of trees and waist-high bushes and brush. However, the immediate area around the shanty was clean and neat. Monique approached the front door, and summoning courage, she drew in several deep breaths, then released them slowly. With steely resolve, she knocked on the door.

"Who is it?" a deep voice called out.

"It's Monique Santori." She was appalled that her voice cracked due to her nerves. She cleared her throat and tried again. "It's Monique, Mystique Santori's daughter."

The door swung inward, and Jacque LeBlanc gazed at her with curious green eyes. She'd forgotten what a big man he was. Her head only reached his shoulders. He was well-built with big shoulders and slim waist and hips.

"Miss Santori, what can I do for you?" he asked.

"Uh…could I come in and speak with you for a few minutes?" She couldn't help but notice that his facial features were bold and chiseled, and his thick, long dark hair was pulled back at the nape of his neck, exposing his strong jawline. The man was definitely hot—not that she cared a bit about what he looked like.

"Speak to me about what?" he asked.

He didn't look particularly friendly and that made her even more nervous. Maybe this was all a big mistake. "I'd like to speak to you about my mother's murder," she said.

"I'm afraid I can't help you. What little information I had, I gave to the chief of police," he replied. "So I'll just tell you good night." He started to close his door.

"Please wait, Mr. LeBlanc." To her horror, she burst into tears.

JACQUE STARED AT the weeping petite young woman. He'd never been able to stand to see a woman cry. He had no idea what was really going on with her or what she wanted from him, but he opened his door wider to invite her inside.

He motioned her toward his sofa where she sank down and drew several audible deep breaths. He sat in a chair facing her.

"I'm sorry. I… I'm so embarrassed," she said as she quickly swiped the tears from her cheeks.

"No reason to be embarrassed," he replied. "I'm just not sure why you're here or what you want from me. As I told you, I gave the police all the information I had concerning your mother's murder."

She gazed at him for several long moments. There was no question that Monique Santori was a beautiful woman. Long dark hair cascaded down her back, and her facial features were soft, yet well-defined. Her eyes were a rich chocolate brown with long dark lashes. She was clad in blue jeans that hugged her legs, and a red blouse that clung to her breasts and cinched at the waist. The color looked great on her.

But what the hell was she doing here?

"Mr. LeBlanc, I need a friend…an educated friend, and it's obvious you are that." She gestured toward his large bookcase, which held a variety of books on different topics.

He stared at her in stunned surprise. She was here because she needed a friend? "Miss Santori, I'm sure you have plenty of intelligent friends, including your two sisters."

"But I don't. My sisters are really the only friends I have, and I can't take my thoughts to them. I need somebody to bounce some ideas off of, and I believe you are that person. And please, make it Monique." There was a definite plea in her eyes.

"What kind of ideas are you talking about?" he asked rather gruffly. The last thing he wanted was to be pulled into some kind of family drama. He liked his relatively solitary life, and he certainly didn't need a new "friend."

"Ideas on how to catch my mother's killer." She leaned forward, and now her eyes filled with a fierce determination. "As I'm sure you know, nobody has been arrested for the crime so far, and right now there are no suspects. The case has stalled…it's on its way to becoming a cold case."

"Miss Sant—I mean Monique, you need to leave the investigation to the law enforcement officials," he replied firmly.

"I've left it to them for almost four months, and now I'm tired of leaving it up to them. I have a plan, but I need to know if you think it's smart. I need somebody to know what I'm doing in the event that something goes wrong."

"If there's even the smallest possibility that something can go wrong, then it's not a good plan," he replied. "Go home, Monique. Go home and don't get involved in all this." He got up from the chair where he'd been sitting and walked to the front door, letting her know not so subtly that he was finished with the conversation.

She frowned and slowly stood. "So you aren't interested in helping me?"

"No, and you need to go home and forget whatever plan you might have," he replied.

She walked to the door. She suddenly looked small and vulnerable, and he nearly broke down and told her to sit back down.

But he didn't, and once she was gone, he released a deep sigh of relief and returned to his chair. Why on earth would she think he would be her new friend? They'd had no interaction at all before this evening. It was all very strange.

Besides, he didn't do friends. Oh, he was fairly friendly with the other gator-hunters and fishermen in the swamp, but he had no real close friends, and that was the way he liked it.

The last thing he wanted to do was to care deeply for anyone. Been there, done that and got the heartbreak that had nearly destroyed him.

As memories of his past life threatened to rear up, he got up from his chair and grabbed the fishing pole and can of worms that sat on a table on his large back porch. He needed to do something to keep the memories at bay.

Thankfully he could fish in a large pool of water mere yards from his back door.

He followed a narrow path down to the water's edge and then sat on the bank and baited his hook. He cast out and then settled in to wait for a bite. When he was out here, it was difficult to think of anything else except the beauty that surrounded him. The reflection of the tall trees in the water was perfect for an artist's brush to capture.

A blue heron swooped in and plucked a small fish out of the water. Despite the competition for fish, Jacque couldn't help but admire the big bird's regal beauty as it continued on its low flight across the water.

His thoughts went to the conversation he'd had with Monique Santori. How desperate she must be to show up at his shanty. He wasn't exactly known for his friendliness around town. For the most part he kept to himself and didn't invite conversations with others. He was definitely an unlikely choice as a new friend.

He fished for about two hours and caught three nice-size fish, a bass and two catfish. He put them in a basket that floated just under the water's surface. He would retrieve them some time tomorrow, still fresh, and they would make a nice dinner or two.

Most of the fishermen in the area sold their fish, but Jacque had no need for money. The only recurring bill he had was for his cell phone, and the only other things he needed to pay for was gasoline for his generator and food. He'd had a healthy savings account of his own when he'd left his home in Baton Rouge for the swamp. Jacque had also inherited a sizable estate from his father, who had died a very wealthy man and named his only son as the sole beneficiary.

In truth, Jacque had more money than he would ever spend in his lifetime. He used a lot of it to support a couple of his favorite charities: one for children with cancer and another a no-kill dog shelter.

It was late afternoon the next day when Jacque pulled six children's books from his book case and set them on the table. Four years ago, if anyone would have told him he would be living in a swamp and teaching reading to five big, burly men, he would have told them they were positively out of their mind. Yet, here he was, doing just that.

It had started when George Trahan, a fellow gator-hunter had confessed to Jacque that he didn't know how to read or write and he wished he could. Jacque had offered to help him and George had readily agreed.

When George had arrived for his first lesson, he'd brought with him Louis Theriot, a fisherman who was also eager to learn to read.

Within two weeks, there were a total of five men who showed up once a week. Jacque had ordered a bunch of supplies, including workbooks and flashcards for the lessons. He was surprised by how fulfilling he found it. In a life with no real purpose, he felt as if he was at least giving a little something back to the place where he lived.

He retrieved the fish he'd caught the day before, cleaned them and fried a couple of pieces for dinner. While he ate, he played music on his phone.

Where once there had been conversation and laughter during meals, there was now only an endless silence that sometimes proved to be too much for him. That was when he would turn on his phone and listen to instrumental music. He'd tried country and western and rock, but the last thing he wanted to hear about was unrequited love or loss.

Off and on all day long, his thoughts had been of Monique. What kind of a plan did she think she had to catch the cold-blooded killer who had slashed her mother's throat? How desperate was she to come to him, of all people, for help?

He just hoped she didn't do anything to get herself into trouble.

It was a little while before dusk when his "students" began to roll in. George was always the first to arrive. He was an affable man dealing with the heartache of finding out that, almost three months before, his fiancée had nearly murdered Angelique Santori in a fit of jealous rage.

George had briefly dated Angelique, and when the two of them broke up, George had fallen in love with a woman named Desiree Augustine. However, he continued to hold Angelique in high regard, something Desiree couldn't stand.

Unbeknownst to George, one night Desiree had gone to Angelique's shanty and tried to stab Angelique to death. It was only when Daniel arrived at the shanty that the attack was halted and Desiree arrested. However, since that time George had become a bit more subdued.

He'd just taken a seat at the table when Louis Theriot and Oliver LeBoeuf, both fishermen, arrived. Minutes later Bill Stanger, a busboy at the café, and Abe Moberly, a dishwasher at the same café arrived, making it a full house.

The men were not only interested in learning how to read but also wanted to learn how to write. They had all admitted that there had been times they'd been embarrassed by their lack of knowledge, and they all wanted to better their lives.

Once they settled in, Jacque handed them each a piece of lined paper. At the top of the paper, Jacque had written their names, and he set them to work copying their names over and over again.

They did that for a little while and then moved on to reading out loud from the children's books. In total, they worked for a little over an hour and a half, and then the men lost their focus and were done for the evening. Besides, twilight had fallen and night quickly approached. The fishermen in the group would be ready to leave and get to their fishing holes.

He walked them all to his front door and stepped outside to see them off. As they all disappeared into the twilight and before he could go back inside, Monique surprised him by stepping out of the deep shadows next to his shanty.

"Mr. LeBlanc, could I please speak with you?" She approached where he stood.

"I don't think we have anything to talk about," he replied, shocked that she was here once again.

She stopped walking when she was right in front of him. She stood close enough to him that he could smell her scent. It was the fragrance of fresh flowers with a hint of something spicy, and it was extremely appealing.

She was clad in a pair of jeans and a navy blouse that cinched at her slender waist and clung to her full breasts. Her hair was pulled into a high ponytail, and she looked quite lovely, not that it mattered. In truth, the fact that he had even noticed her attractiveness at all irritated him.

"I didn't get a chance last night to tell you that I have a little money saved up, and I actually want to hire you." Her beautiful eyes held not only a plea but also a profound grief that touched something deep inside him despite his desire not to get involved. "It would just be for brainstorming purposes," she added hurriedly. "All you would need to do is talk with me, and I'll pay you for your thoughts. Please, Mr. LeBlanc, won't you help me?"

"You wouldn't have to pay me," he replied gruffly.

It was at that moment, against his better judgment, he realized he was going to help her.

Chapter Two

It was Monique's day off. A blessing, since she'd been up half the night writing down every single thing she knew so far about the murder investigation and all the questions she wanted to bounce off Jacque.

Jacque. He was brusque and more than a little bit intimidating, but he'd surprised her by finally agreeing to talk with her last night. He'd agreed to meet her today at two.

Soon after Monique had gotten back to her own shanty last night, Angelique had called. Her voice was filled with joy as she told Monique that Daniel had indeed proposed to her. Monique had a feeling it wouldn't be long before Luke proposed to Dominique.

Monique was thrilled that both her sisters had found their forever love, but she liked her quiet single life. She enjoyed her job and occasionally liked going to the Voodoo Lounge, a bar with a large dance floor. She'd always gone there with her sisters.

However, since her mother's murder, she hadn't felt much like dancing.

She ate a light lunch of salad and a handful of cooked shrimp. As she cleaned up the kitchen, her nerves jumped in the pit of her stomach as she thought about meeting with Jacque once again. She'd wished for this, and now that it was actually happening, she only hoped Jacque could help her get the answers and the clarity she sought.

It was close to two when she left her shanty. She wore a light yellow sundress with a bright poppy print. It was cool and comfortable as she walked the trail that would take her to Jacque's shanty.

Last night when she'd first arrived at his place, she'd heard the sound of men talking and laughing inside. She'd stood in the deep shadows next to his shanty, and it wasn't long after that when five men had left his place.

A social visit? That certainly didn't fit with what she knew about Jacque. According to everything she had heard, the man was a loner. She definitely was curious why the other men had been there, but it was really none of her business.

As his shanty came into view, she clutched her notebook, where she'd written everything she knew about the murder, close to her chest. There was something they all were missing in the investigation, and somehow, she needed to figure it out. At the moment she didn't even have any suspects in mind, but she was hoping with Jacque's help, she could identify a potential murderer. With this thought in mind, she knocked firmly on his front door.

He opened the door and greeted her rather curtly. "I thought we could sit at the table for this brainstorming session," he said and gestured her toward the kitchen area.

She noticed he already had a notebook and pen on the table. She also couldn't help but notice that he looked quite handsome in a pair of jeans and a green-and-black-striped short-sleeved dress shirt. His hair was tied back, and the green in the shirt made the bright color of his eyes more intense.

She hadn't really looked around his shanty the night before but now she took note of how attractive and spotlessly clean it was. The sofa and chair were a dark gray with a couple of light gray throw pillows. A potbellied stove stood in the corner of the living area with a large green plant spilling its vines and leaves over the top and down the sides. A large bookcase stretched across one wall, filled with books of all kinds. Beneath her feet, there was a large gray area rug with yellow flecks, a nice pop of color. Everything was neat and tidy, a very attractive space.

"Can I get you something to drink?" His question broke through her thoughts as she sank onto a chair at the wooden kitchen table and set her notebook down.

"No, thanks, I'm fine." She dug into her purse to retrieve a pen, then dropped the purse to the floor next to her chair. There was a back door near where she sat, and in a quick glance, she took in a neatly cleared path that led to a body of water in the near distance.

He sat across from her and looked at her expectantly. Instantly her nerves rose up inside her. "How are you this evening, Mr. LeBlanc?" she asked.

"I'm fine, but we aren't here to small talk or socialize," he replied curtly.

She cleared her throat and began. She told him everything she knew about the murder itself and then spoke about the fact that the police had initially fixated on a single suspect.

Pierre Guidry had been her mother's lover for years.

They would break up for months at a time, but they always found their way back to each other. However, at the time of Mystique's murder, they had been broken up. The authorities had believed Pierre showed up the night of the murder to get back with her. Presumably, Mystique hadn't wanted to resume a relationship with him, and law enforcement's theory was that a fight had ensued, ending with Pierre killing her.

Unfortunately, they had no real evidence to prove this theory.

"I know he was finally cleared by Lucien Rousseau who saw Pierre out in the swamp fishing at the time of the murder," Jacque said.

She nodded. "And since that time the investigation has completely stalled."

"So what exactly do you want from me?" he asked with a frown.

She could smell his scent in the air. Shaving cream and soap mixed with a woodsy cologne she found quite appealing. "I want you to help me find some suspects. You do realize my mother's client book was also stolen on the night of the murder," she added.

"I heard something about that." He frowned. "If it was my investigation, that would be where most of my energy would be focused. Who would want that book enough to be willing to kill for it?"

"That's what I'm hoping you could help me figure out," she replied. "I know Daniel has spoken to a lot of people who were seeing my mother for one reason or another."

Jacque's frown deepened, the gesture not taking anything away from his handsomeness. "I don't believe the killer is anyone from the swamp," he said. "Nobody who lives here has much to lose if their secrets got out."

She looked at him in surprise. He was probably right, and this was the exact reason she needed his input. As far as she knew, nobody in law enforcement had thought about ruling out the people from the swamp…people who had so little to lose.

"So the killer is from town." She opened her notebook and picked up her pen.

"And is probably fairly prominent," he added. "Who do you know for sure is from town and visited your mother?"

"My mother often went to Lucinda Reese's home to meet with her. Lucinda is wealthy and extremely well-respected. But there's no way I believe that she killed my mother."

"Why not?" His sharp gaze pinned her in place.

"For one thing she's an older woman. The reason my mother went to her house was because Lucinda was too physically frail to make the trek to Mama's shanty."

"Do you know why Lucinda was seeing your mother?" Monique shook her head. "No."

"Does Lucinda have sons…or maybe some grandsons who would do her bidding?" he asked.

"She has two sons, but they don't live here in town," Monique replied. "I'm still not convinced she had anything to do with this. Maybe we just need to make a list of all the prominent men in town because I truly believe my mother was killed by a man." Pain once again stabbed through her as she thought of her beautiful mother's throat slashed. It had been such a heinous killing.

Jacque picked up his pen. "Then let's start with the mayor. Do you know if he was seeing your mother?"

"I don't know. I don't think anybody knows for sure who was seeing her." She wrote down Ralph Dupree. The mayor of Dark Waters would certainly have a lot to lose if an embarrassing or political bombshell of some kind came out.

For the next hour, they threw out names of potential suspects. By the time they finished, she had fourteen names written in her notebook.

"This is a good starting place," she said.

"Do you now intend to take the list to Daniel?" he asked. He leaned back in his chair, appearing to command the space around him, a strong masculine energy wafting from him.

"No, now I begin to do my own sleuthing," she replied.

He immediately leaned forward, his green eyes glowing with the intensity of a laser as he focused on her. "What exactly does that mean?"

"I intend to go to each of these men's homes and snoop around for my mother's book. If I see it in somebody's home, then I know that person is the killer," she replied.

"Are you out of your mind?" he snapped and straightened in his chair. "A reckless stunt like that could get you killed."

Warmth leaped into her cheeks and she raised her chin defiantly. "Jacque, I can be very sneaky when I need to be."

His gaze turned skeptical. "And what ruse do you intend to use to get into these houses to snoop around?"

Once again, her cheeks grew warm under his penetrating scrutiny. Lord, but the man had beautiful eyes. She would love to see them lit up by his smile. But so far, he hadn't offered her even a hint of one, and his eyes remained like hard emeralds.

"I haven't quite figured that part out yet," she admitted with a frown. "It might take me a day or two, but I'll come up with something. Then once I'm inside, I'll ask to use the restroom, and that's when I'm hoping to do a little snooping in the bedrooms in search of my mother's book. I figure her book is either in a bookcase or in somebody's bedroom drawer."

"It's a bad plan," he said.

"It's a good plan," she countered firmly.

"You should take this list to the police and stay out of things."

"I'm tired of leaving things up to the police." She shut her notebook and looked back at him once again. "I keep repeating that it's been almost four months, and now they don't even have a suspect." These words had become her mantra, her reminder of time passing with no relief in sight. "I have to do something," she said fervently.

She leaned toward him as tears pressed hot behind her eyelids. "Don't you understand? I can't get past my grief. I'm stuck in it. I don't eat, and my sleep is disturbed by nightmares of the murder. The only thing that's going to help me get on with my life is to get her killer under arrest." She sat back in her chair once again. "Look, Mr. LeBlanc, I really appreciate you helping me with this. I told you I'd pay you for your time, so what do I owe you?"

He stared at her for a long moment and then released a deep sigh. "You might as well call me Jacque, and you don't owe me anything. Partners don't pay partners."

"Partners?" She gazed at him hopefully.

He gave her a curt nod. "I can't let you do this all alone. If you really intend to do this, then you need some backup."

"I really intend to do this," she replied adamantly.

"Then I have a ruse that will get you inside and potentially into whatever room these men keep their books," he replied.

"And what ruse is that?" she asked curiously. Her heartbeat quickened its rhythm with excitement. This was far better than she had hoped for.

"I've been teaching some of the men around here how to read and write. We could go to these houses and ask for donations of books."

"That would be perfect," she replied, her excitement growing. "And it's wonderful that you're teaching some of the men how to read and write. I know there are many in the swamp who didn't go to school for one reason or another."

"These men are motivated and have often been embarrassed by not being about to read something or sign their own name," he replied.

"Needing books is a perfect reason to get us into these homes. So are you really going to be my partner in all this?" Once again, she looked at him hopefully.

"That's what I said."

"I want us to get started as soon as possible, but I won't be available tomorrow. I work until nine, and that would be too late to go to anyone's home. But the day after tomorrow, I work the morning shift and get off at two. That will give us plenty of time to visit a few people. That is, if you're available then," she quickly added.

"I'm available. So day after tomorrow, I'll meet you at your shanty around two thirty." He scooted his chair back, indicating he was finished with the conversation.

She grabbed her purse from the floor and dropped her pen inside it, then stood and once again gripped her notebook close to her chest. The night had gone far better than she'd ever imagined. She couldn't believe he'd agreed to team up with her.

Together they walked to his front door. Once there, she turned back to him. "Mr. Le… Jacque, I can't thank you enough for agreeing to help me."

"I would prefer you stay out of the investigation. But if you are going to do this, you need to have somebody with you," he replied . He opened the door.

"Could you do me just one more favor before I leave?" she asked, hoping she wasn't about to shoot herself in the foot.

"What's that?"

"Could you smile?"

He looked at her in what appeared to be stunned surprise. "Why is that necessary?"

She smiled up at him. "Call me crazy, but I think people who are working as partners should smile at one another. You know, it isn't hard to do. You just turn that frown upside down."

He stared at her for a long moment, and then he grinned. It was a transformative smile, softening the hard lines of his face and warming up the beautiful green of his eyes. It lasted only a moment and then fell away. "I have a feeling you can be quite a handful," he said.

"Trust me, I'll behave." Her own smile faded. "This mission is far too important to take lightly. Thank you again, Jacque, and I'll see you day after tomorrow." With that, she walked out of the door.

As she headed back to her cabin, a sweet anticipation swept through her. It was possible within a matter of days she would be able to name her mother's killer.

However, there was no question that she had a bit of apprehension in working with Jacque. She knew nothing about the man or what had originally brought him to the swamp. She was trusting the word of a stranger.

She just hoped she wasn't making a wrong decision in involving him. What she planned to do was already risky enough. She was on the hunt for a cold-blooded killer.

Jacque sank down in his easy chair and thought about the woman who had just left. There was no question that she was a pretty little thing. With her long dark hair and big dark eyes, she'd looked stunning in the yellow-and-red sundress she'd had on. And she'd smelled like a field of summer flowers with a hint of spice.

However, Jacque wasn't moved by a woman's beauty or the attractive scent of her skin. There was nothing about another woman that would ever move him again.

It had definitely surprised him when she'd asked him to smile. When he had, it had felt foreign to his mouth and had made him realize in the past four years he had rarely smiled.

Monique Santori was the least likely person to go after a killer. Most of the reason he'd agreed to help her was because he feared if left to her own devices, she'd wind up hurt or dead.

If she saw her mother's book in one of the homes, there was nothing that would keep the killer from murdering her. As much as he didn't want to get involved, he also didn't want to see her get herself in trouble.

There had been a fierceness in the depths of her eyes, mingling with a wealth of grief that made him realize with or without him, she intended to follow through on her plan.

What he should do was take her intentions to Daniel. However, he didn't think even a strong talking to from the chief of police would stop her. What she had planned wasn't exactly illegal, so Daniel couldn't lock her up to keep her safe.

He released a deep sigh. He still didn't know why she'd come to him. They hadn't been social with each other at all in the past. Hell, they hadn't even been passing acquaintances.

Of course, everyone in the swamp knew of the voodoo queen, Mystique, and her three beautiful daughters. Mystique's murder had definitely shaken up everyone in Dark Waters. It had been a particularly atrocious crime for the small town.

Some of the people in the swamp had feared the powerful Mystique dabbled in black magic and would come back to life with a vengeance and would curse all those who had come to her for a charm or a spell.

Then there were the others…the ones who feared that the secrets they'd spilled to Mystique under the cover of night would come to light now that she was dead. And those were the men Monique wanted to visit…and one of them was potentially a killer.

He was hoping that by the day after tomorrow she would change her mind about the whole thing. Maybe she would take the list they'd created and any other thoughts she had to the chief of police. That would be the smart thing to do.

Jacque knew how hard Daniel was working on the case. The lawman had come to speak to him right after the murder. He'd heard the rumor that Jacque knew a lot of what went on in the swamp.

It was true that Jacque kept his ear to the ground. Teaching the five men, he heard a lot of gossip as they talked with each other before and after the lessons. However, he'd heard nothing salient about Mystique's murder.

With his thoughts still racing, he got up from his chair. He fried up some fish for dinner and then cleaned up the kitchen.

The conversation with Monique had gone on much longer than he'd initially intended. He sank back down in his chair and tried to read for a little while, but his conversation with Monique kept replaying in his head.

Hopefully his mind would quiet enough so he could sleep. Even though it was a little early for his bedtime, he was tired. He turned off all the lanterns that were lit in the room except one, which he carried with him into his bedroom.

He set the lantern on one of the two nightstands and then turned down the navy blue spread on the king-size bed. He stripped off his clothes until he was only in a pair of boxers and then he climbed into bed and turned the lantern off.

Bright moonlight drifted in the window, and frogs croaked good night from the nearby pond. Insects clicked and buzzed, adding their songs to the lullaby of the night. It wasn't long before he drifted off to sleep.

HE AWAKENED EARLY the next morning and grabbed a towel from the closet in his bathroom. He went out on his back porch where a wooden shower stall stood.

If there was one thing he missed from his former life, it was a good, strong shower. The shower in the swamp consisted of sun-warmed rain water that trickled from a complicated structure of pipes, ultimately creating a rather weak spray. Still, it was enough to get him clean.

He took a quick shower and washed his hair, then wrapped a towel around his waist to go back inside the house. Once in his bedroom, he pulled on a clean pair of jeans and one of his short-sleeved dress shirts.

Brushing out his long hair, he decided that today was the day he was going into town to get a haircut. He'd been thinking about it for weeks. He was tired of caring for it, and he'd never really wanted long hair to begin with. It had been part laziness and part aversion of going into town that had kept him from visiting the barber for so long.

He returned to the back porch to start his generator, which would give him enough electricity to charge his phone, make breakfast and brew a pot of coffee.

Once the coffee was brewing, he put a half dozen strips of bacon to fry in an iron skillet on the electric stovetop. Within minutes, the smell of coffee and frying bacon filled the shanty.

Once it was ready, he poured himself a cup of coffee, flipped the bacon strips over and then sank down at the table to wait for the bacon to get done. Immediately his thoughts filled with Monique.

Was she having second thoughts about her plan? He

hoped she was going to the chief of police instead of to a house to hunt for a stolen book and a stone-cold killer.

He got up and took the bacon out of the skillet and then fried two eggs and made toast. Once he was finished with breakfast, he cleaned up the kitchen and then decided to take his pirogue out to do a little gator gazing.

Even though he had no intention of hunting today, he went into the bedroom and pulled his shoulder holster and revolver out of the top drawer of his dresser. He never went out in the swamp without his firearm. Armed with his gun and his cell phone, he got into the shallow boat and took off.

It was beautiful at this time of the morning. The sky was an intense blue overhead, and the sun reflected in the water. Birds sang from the tops of the trees, and fish jumped as if to taunt him.

Using his push pole, he left the shore and then used a paddle to gently glide across the water. The air smelled of the many plants and trees, and he drew in deep breaths of the fresh air tinged with the faint odor of decay. He'd grown accustomed to the latter smell since it was always present in the swamp.

In the distance he saw a large gator sunning on top of a fallen log while a smaller gator swam in the water with only his eyes showing his presence. He knew they wouldn't bother him as long as he didn't bother them.

Four years ago, he'd arrived in the Dark Waters swamp a broken man with little will to live. He'd had no fear of anything, including the big gators that lived so close to his shanty. That was when he'd decided to become a gator-hunter…a foolish job for a man with no fear.

Lately he had no desire to catch one of the big beasts.

He much preferred the peacefulness of fishing or just sightseeing in the swamp that still held so many of nature's mysteries for him to discover. He'd learned to seek peace wherever he could.

So why the hell had he agreed to help Monique with her crazy scheme?

Deep down in his bones, he knew why. It was the yawning grief that had darkened her beautiful eyes. Despite her attractive floral scent, the smell of deep grief clung to her.

He knew that kind of grief. It was an old friend of his and one that he wouldn't wish on anyone. If he could help her alleviate some of her grief, it would be worth it. The only thing that had helped him was time, but obviously she wasn't in the mood to wait any longer.

At two twenty the next day, Jacque left his shanty and took off walking down the narrow path to Monique's place. He knew where most of the people in the swamp lived. He'd made it his business to know when he first moved here.

It was another warm summer day. As he walked, something scurried in the bushes at the side of the path, but he didn't see what kind of little animal it was. The swamp was home to so many small creatures.

He was still hoping he'd get to her shanty and she'd tell him she'd changed her mind and was taking the new list of suspects to Daniel.

But just in case she hadn't, he wore his gun. He'd keep it on each time they went to one of the houses in town. If she was really going through with her scheme, then he intended to do everything in his power to make sure she stayed safe. Hopefully, after visiting one or two homes, she would realize the futility and potential danger she was entertaining and she would stop.

He finally arrived at her shanty and went up the bridge that led to the front door. Once there, he knocked, and she answered almost immediately.

"Hi, Jacque, come on in," she said with one of her wide-open smiles. She looked very pretty in a long red-and-white-striped skirt and a crisp, tailored white blouse. Red beads hung around her neck and matched the earrings in her ears. "I just need to grab my purse and take care of a few things, then I'll be ready to go. Feel free to have a seat." She gestured toward the navy sofa with bright yellow throw pillows.

As she disappeared into what he assumed was her bedroom, he looked around the shanty. Along with the sofa, there was a matching chair, a potbellied stove in one corner and a small bookcase against one wall.

There were pops of yellow everywhere. A small arrangement of navy and yellow artificial flowers set on one of the shelves. Pictures of yellow flowers hung on the walls. It all made the space feel cheerful and bright.

He was only seated for a couple of minutes before she returned to the room, this time with a red purse with a long strap over her shoulder. "Ready?" she asked. Her features radiated with sudden surprise. "Wait...you cut your hair."

"I didn't cut it, but the barber did yesterday." He stood.

She openly studied him for a long moment. "It looks quite nice," she replied. "Now, are we ready to go?"

"Are you really sure you want to do this?" he asked.

Her chin went up a notch. "Positive. All we need to figure out now is am I driving or are you?"

"I'll drive. You can navigate." At least that way he'd be in control if they needed to get away from someplace fast.

"Then let's go." She followed him out the door, pausing a moment to lock it before heading down the bridge.

He took the lead, walking on the path that would take them to where his car was parked just outside the swamp's entrance.

Despite all the other scents that the swamp brought, he could still smell her attractive floral fragrance. He wasn't sure why it appealed to him so much.

It didn't take them long to break through the jungle-like growth and into the area where people who lived in the swamp parked their cars.

He led her to his, a silver convertible Mustang. There were still nights when the silence of his life grew too heavy and deep. On some of those nights, he put the top down on his car, turned up the music and just drove.

"Nice ride," she said as he opened the passenger door.

"Thanks," he replied. "I like it."

"I've arranged the visits by areas of town," she said once they were both settled in his car.

"All you need to do is point me in the right direction," he replied as he started the engine.

"Head to Main Street, then take a left," she said. "The first stop on my list is the mayor's house."

"It's early in the day. He'll still be in his office at City Hall." He tightened his grip on the steering wheel, dreading this whole thing.

"It doesn't matter if he's home or not. I'm hoping his wife will be there and will let us in." He felt her gaze on him. "Thank you, Jacque, for your help."

He flashed her a quick glance. "I'm helping you, but I still don't approve of any of this."

"I can tell that by the frown you're wearing," she replied. He looked back at the road as she continued, "You do realize you might need to look a little more pleasant when you talk with people about your need for books."

"I'll do the best I can," he replied.

"Maybe you could start by practicing with me," she added.

He couldn't help the small laugh that escaped him. It startled him. He couldn't remember the last time he'd actually laughed out loud.

"Oh, that's so much better," she said with obvious delight.

He frowned once again. It was at that moment Jacque realized she was shaking up the insular, private life he'd built for himself. Monique Santori was potentially the real danger to him in this situation.

Chapter Three

Monique had been nervous from the moment Jacque walked in her shanty's door. He'd looked even bigger and more powerful than she'd ever seen him. It didn't hurt that over his short-sleeved sky-blue dress shirt he wore a holster with a gun. Many men wore guns in Dark Waters, which had an open carry policy.

While the gun made her feel protected, it also reminded her that what she planned to do could be dangerous. Even the fact that she'd gotten him to laugh didn't staunch the nerves that roared inside her.

The neat, short haircut emphasized the bold lines of his face, making him even more handsome. She could once again smell his scent. It was all clean male and some woodsy fragrance she found so appealing.

"We need to get our story straight," she said. "And turn right at the next street."

"I know my part of the story. I'm teaching some men in the swamp to learn to read and I'm looking for book donations. So what's your story? Why are you with me?"

"We met in the swamp one day and got to talking. You told me about what you were doing, and I instantly wanted to help you," she replied. "By the way, I want to tell you again that I think it's quite admirable…what you're doing for the men."

"They're all eager to learn, and I'm happy to help them out," he replied.

"Mama insisted we go to school. She impressed upon us how important a good education was," she said. "Turn left on the next street, and Ralph's house is the second one on the right."

The Dupree home was a large ranch house painted in a deep blue with white shutters. Jacque pulled into the driveway and parked. The front porch held a couple of chairs and a small round table, making it appear quite inviting.

"Ralph's wife's name is Heidi."

"So you know her?" Jacque asked.

"Yes, she comes into the dress shop fairly frequently. I have to admit, working at All That Jazz has given me the opportunity to know most of the women in town."

He turned off the engine, and they both unbuckled their seat belts. "Are you really ready for this?" he asked.

Her heart quickened as tension coiled tight inside her. "As ready as I'll ever be."

Together they got out of the car and headed for the front door. "Here we go," she murmured as he knocked.

He had to knock twice before the door was opened by Heidi. The mayor's wife was in her late forties. She was an attractive redhead who, along with her husband, Ralph, was very well-liked by the people in Dark Waters.

"Monique," she said in surprise and then looked quizzically at Jacque, who quickly introduced himself.

"Hi, Heidi. Could we come in and talk to you for just

a few minutes? I promise we won't take up too much of your time," Monique said.

"Of course, please come in." Heidi opened the door wider to allow them entry.

They walked into a large living room that held an oversize blue floral sofa and matching love seat. An enormous television hung on one wall and a huge china cabinet filled with fragile-looking figurines and beautiful dishes sat on the other.

"Please, have a seat and tell me what I can do for you." Heidi gestured to the sofa while she sat on the love seat that faced it.

"I've started a program in the swamp," Jacque began.

"Excuse me, but before we get into it…" Monique interrupted and gazed apologetically at Heidi. "I'm so embarrassed but could I use your restroom?"

"Of course, and there's no reason to be embarrassed when nature calls." Heidi got up and walked with Monique to the mouth of a long hallway. "It's the second door on your right."

"Thank you," Monique replied. She hurried down the hallway and went into the bathroom. She only stayed there a moment and then quietly opened the door again.

She could hear Heidi and Jacque talking about the upcoming fall festival that was happening in three weeks. She slid back out of the bathroom and crept farther down the hallway.

She passed a bedroom that appeared to be a guest room. She assumed that if somebody had her mother's book, it would be hidden in a drawer or tucked into a bookcase. But she didn't believe it would be kept in a guest bedroom.

The primary bedroom was on the left at the end of the hallway. It was easily identified by the alarm clock on one of the nightstands and the collection of women's perfume and men's cologne on the top of the dresser. This room also had an en suite bathroom, further identifying it as where the couple slept.

She quickly pulled out drawers in the dresser and in the nightstands, checking all through them for the missing dark blue hardback notebook.

Not finding it in there, she stepped out into the hallway and had only taken a step or two forward when Heidi appeared. "Wha…what are you doing, Monique?" she asked with a curious wrinkle dancing in the center of her forehead.

"I'm so sorry," Monique released a small laugh. "I walked out of the bathroom and got completely turned around. I didn't realize my mistake until I got down here."

Heidi laughed. "Just follow me, and I'll take you back to the living room."

As Monique walked behind her, she thanked her lucky stars that she hadn't been caught riffling through the drawers. Still, nerves tightened her stomach at the close call. She couldn't imagine what Heidi would have done if she had caught Monique red-handed in her bedroom.

"She got lost," Heidi said to Jacque, who visibly relaxed at the sight of Monique.

"I'm bad with the directions inside a house, imagine how bad it is when I get behind the wheel of my car. That's why Jacque is driving today," Monique said with another small laugh as she once again took her seat on the sofa next to him.

"Mr. LeBlanc has been sharing with me the new project he has going in the swamp. I'm definitely all in for literacy no matter where it takes place. I'm assuming you're here for a donation. Just let me go get my purse."

"Actually, Mrs. Dupree, we aren't here for any money donations. What we would like is any books you could give us for the men to use," Jacque said.

"Oh, I'm sure I can help you out with that. If you both want to follow me, in one of the bedrooms we have a bookcase where we keep what books we have."

Jacque and Monique followed her down the hallway to the last room on the right. Monique had only quickly glanced into the room when she'd been snooping. She hadn't noticed the small bookcase on the wall behind the door. She'd have to do better in the future.

Heidi began pulling out books and handing them to Jacque. Monique stood next to him and scrutinized all the books on the shelves, seeking the one she was desperate to find. But it wasn't there.

By the time Heidi was finished, Jacque had eight hardback books in his arms. "I hope that helps," she said as the three of them walked back up the hall and into the living room.

"Thank you, Heidi. You've been very generous," Monique said.

"Yes, thank you so much, Mrs. Dupree," Jacque added.

"And now we'll just get out of your hair." Monique walked to the front door with Jacque following close behind her. "And don't forget I have that new shipment of your favorite brand coming into the store on Wednesday," she added.

"Trust me, I haven't forgotten. I'll be at the store bright

and early on Wednesday morning with my credit card in hand," Heidi said with a wide grin.

Moments later Monique and Jacque reached his car in the driveway. He placed the books in his back seat, then got in behind the steering wheel. "That was a close call," he said.

"It was," Monique agreed. "I was totally freaked out when she caught me down the hallway."

"Thank God you're a fast thinker and a good actress," he replied.

"I think we need to come up with a way for you to do something to warn me if somebody comes looking for me."

"I think you need to forget about this whole thing," he replied with a scowl.

"Jacque, despite the close call, we did it. And I can now cross Ralph Dupree off my list of suspects," she said. "I don't believe he has my mama's book. Maybe you could have a coughing fit and that would warn me that somebody is coming."

He glanced over at her, the near-neon green of his eyes seeming to pierce right through her. "Are you willfully ignoring the fact that I just said I think you should forget about this plan and leave things to the authorities?"

"Yes, I'm willfully ignoring you," she replied. She reached out and wrapped her fingers around his wrist on the gear shift. His skin was invitingly warm. "Please, Jacque, I want you as my partner, but I don't want you as a doubting Thomas. I need you to be one hundred percent in with me on this." She withdrew her hand.

He stared at her for another long minute and then put

his car into gear to back out of the Dupree driveway. "So who are we seeing next?"

Monique breathed a sigh of relief. There was no question that she felt better with Jacque by her side. She would have been far more nervous if she was trying to do this all on her own.

"Next on the list is Judge Waylan Frankel's home. Take a right when you come to the end of the street."

They didn't speak anymore other than her giving him directions.

He finally reached the judge's home and parked in the driveway. "This is going to be more difficult for you since it's a two-story," he said.

"You're right." She frowned as she stared at the large home. It was definitely going to be difficult for her to get away and go upstairs to search. If she got caught upstairs, she wouldn't be able to use the excuse that she'd gotten turned around.

"We'll see how things go. Judge Frankel should still be at work. His wife's name is Isabelle, and she's always been quite pleasant when she comes into the store."

Nearly an hour later they left the Frankel home. Monique hadn't been able to search the upstairs. She was about to ask to use the restroom and sneak upstairs when the judge had gotten home from work.

He had greeted them and then gone upstairs to change into more casual clothes. However, there was a large bookcase in the judge's study, and Isabelle had invited them into the room so she could donate some books.

As she'd pulled out half a dozen books, Monique carefully scanned the shelf. Her mother's book wasn't there. Now, back in Jacque's car, she looked at him curiously.

"How about we stop our sleuthing for the night and grab some dinner at the café?"

"I usually don't eat out," he responded.

"Could you maybe force yourself to do it this once?"

"You're a pushy little thing," he replied with a quick glance at her.

"Okay, I might be little and pushy, but I'm not a thing. I'm a woman who doesn't feel like cooking tonight, and I thought it wouldn't hurt for us to share a meal out together since we're partners in subterfuge." She offered him one of her brightest smiles. "Please, Jacque, don't force me to cook for myself tonight."

He smiled then. It was a rueful grin that softened the lines in his face and deepened the green of his eyes. It also caused a surprising spark of warmth to shoot off in the pit of her stomach.

"Far be it for me to force you to cook, so this once I'll go to the café with you. I'm also agreeing to this because I'm starving, and I don't feel like cooking, either."

"Great," she replied. So far, she had only looked at Jacque as a means to an end, but she now was surprised to realize she was hoping to learn a little more about him.

She just hoped it wasn't a mistake to invite the intense, gruff loner any further into her life.

Jacque had no idea why he had agreed to go the café with Monique. Maybe it was because of the brilliance of her smile. Or the inviting warmth and sparkle in her eyes. Maybe it was just because he really was hungry, and like her, he wasn't in the mood to go home and cook something.

"I'm assuming you don't go to the café often," she said.

"You would assume correctly," he replied.

"Why is that?" she asked. Once again, he felt her gaze on him.

"I'm not exactly a social kind of person. Besides, I always have what I need at my shanty, so why go out to eat?" He turned into the parking lot of the café, located at the back of the building.

"It was back here where my sister, Dominique, was kidnapped," she said softly as he pulled into a spot near the big trash dumpster.

He put the car in Park and then turned to gaze at her. "You must have been terrified when that happened."

"We all were," she replied.

"Thank God, she was found safe and sound." He turned off the car engine and unbuckled his seat belt. "It's hard to believe that a respected man who worked for the city was the culprit."

She unfastened her seat belt and turned to look at him once again. "Burt Stanfield hid his twisted obsession with Dominique very well. It just goes to show you that evil exists, and eventually we're going to find the evil person who killed my mother." She smiled at him again, and the force of her beautiful smile lit an unexpected warmth inside him.

"Let's go eat." He broke eye contact and opened his car door. That flicker of warmth that had washed through him had unsettled him.

Together they walked around the building and to the front door. Upon entering into the Dark Water Cafe, he was hit with an onslaught to his senses. The scents of cooking fish, meats and freshly baked bread among other things all made his stomach grumble with hunger. The noise level was definitely more than he was accustomed to with clanking silverware, laughter and conversation coming from all the tables and booths.

He was pleased when Monique spied an empty booth toward the back of the café where it seemed a bit quieter. They slid in facing each other, and almost immediately a waitress joined them.

"Hi, Monique," she greeted.

"Hi, Sunny," she replied and then made the introductions between Sunny and Jaque. She indicated that Sunny was a close friend of Monique's sister, Dominique. Dominique also worked as a waitress in the café but wasn't working this evening.

They both ordered iced tea to drink, and then Sunny left the booth.

"See, isn't this nice?" Monique said to him as she settled back against the dark brown leather of the booth.

"It's okay," he agreed. He plucked the menus out of their holding place between the tall salt and pepper shakers, handed her one and kept one for himself.

Despite the fact that he'd visited the café before, he'd been aware of the curious glances and whispers that followed them as they'd walked to the booth. It had to be a surprise for people to see him in Monique's company. He was sure the gossip mill was already working hard.

"You're going to get a lot of questions after this meal," he said. "You'll have a lot of explaining to do."

She smiled at him. "I'm aware of that, but the answer is really quite simple. I'm working with you on your project in the swamp, and while we were out getting book donations, we got hungry. In any case, I'm allowed to eat with whomever I want, and tonight I chose to eat with you."

Before he could reply, a plump brown-haired woman approached their booth. Everyone in the swamp knew Nola Fontenot. She'd been one of Mystique's closest friends, and she was also one of the town's biggest gossipers.

"Darling Monique, it's always nice to see you out and enjoying life," Nola said. "I know that's what your dear mother would want for you." She turned her attention to Jacque. "Mr. LeBlanc, even though we haven't officially met, I know Mystique thought quite highly of you after the two of you met."

"And I know from talking to her that she thought very highly of you, too," Jacque replied, aware of Monique's curious gaze on him.

"We all miss her so much, and I don't ever think we'll get over it until her killer is identified and thrown in jail where he belongs," Nola replied.

"Hopefully that person is going to be identified sooner rather than later," Monique said.

An obvious sadness filled Nola's eyes. "I don't know how that's going to happen since the police don't even have a suspect in mind."

"There are some of us who are not leaving it up to the police," Monique replied.

Nola stared at her for a long moment. "I hope you aren't doing anything to get yourself in trouble, Monique."

Monique laughed. It was a pleasant, melodious sound. "Oh, you know me, Nola. I'm not the type to get myself into any trouble. I leave that up to my sisters."

Nola smiled at her. "You're right. Oh, and now your drinks have arrived," she said as Sunny stepped up next to the booth. "I'll just leave you two to get on with your dinner."

Sunny set their drinks down and then took their food orders. Monique ordered the seafood platter, and Jacque got the meatloaf special.

"You never told me you personally knew my mother," Monique said the moment Sunny left. Her big brown eyes gazed at him intently. The dark grief was back. It stole the sparkle from her beautiful eyes.

"I only met her one time," he replied. "It was late one night…around midnight, and I was fishing at the spot I have near my shanty. She was out looking for a special flower that only bloomed at night. She surprised me by sitting down on the bank next to me, and we began to chat."

"What did you talk about?" she asked, as if hungry for any nugget of information about the mother she had tragically lost to a killer's hand.

He took a drink of his tea. "At first, she asked me if the fishing was good, and I told her I wasn't catching anything. I was really just out enjoying the peace and quiet of the night. She told me about the flower she was trying to find. It was mostly just small talk. However, she did tell me how much she loved you and your sisters and how proud she was of all of you."

"Thank you," Monique said softly. "That's so nice to hear."

"That was pretty much the end of our time together. She got up and wandered back into the swamp, and eventually I went back to my shanty."

By that time Sunny had arrived with their meals. The

meatloaf special included thick slices of meat, a mound of mashed potatoes and gravy and seasoned green beans.

The food on Monique's plate looked just as appetizing. There were several pieces of golden fried fish and shrimp with sides of macaroni and cheese, cole slaw and cornbread.

"You sure can't complain about the portion sizes here," he said as he picked up his fork.

"That's definitely true. They're more than generous," she agreed. She picked up her fork and speared a shrimp. "Since you cook for yourself most nights, you must be a real talented chef."

Once again, an unexpected small laugh escaped him. "Not hardly," he replied as she popped the shrimp into her mouth. "Most nights I just fry up a panful of fish, and that's dinner. What about you?"

"I enjoy cooking most of the time," she replied. "But only if I'm cooking for somebody."

"Do you have a specialty?"

"My sisters say I make a good chicken and rice with wine sauce," she replied.

"That sounds good," he replied.

For the next few minutes, they fell silent as they focused on eating. However, it wasn't long before they began to talk again.

They talked about music, and she confessed that she loved to go to the Voodoo Lounge and dance. He told her he couldn't remember the last time he'd danced. Small talk. Jacque had nearly forgotten how to do it, but Monique made it easy. They moved on from music to her work at the dress shop. She regaled him with several funny stories about her clients and their clothing choices.

The more they talked, the more uncomfortable he became. He didn't want to get to know her better. He would help her in her search for her mother's book, but that was the beginning and the end of it. He didn't need a new friend, especially not one as attractive as Monique.

"Where are you from, Jacque?" she asked. "I know you aren't swamp born and raised."

"Baton Rouge," he replied.

"What brought you to the swamp?" Her brown eyes were filled with curiosity.

His old friend grief slammed into his chest, and for a moment he struggled to suppress it. He looked down at his plate, his appetite gone. When he looked up at her again, he was back in control.

"I needed a change in my life, and I wanted to go someplace where it would be peaceful. I saw an ad for a shanty for sale. I bought it, and here I am."

"It's quite a big change from Baton Rouge to the swamp," she replied.

"Yeah, it took me a little while to adjust," he admitted. By that time, they were finished eating. "Do you want dessert?" he asked.

"Oh no, I'm stuffed," she replied.

"Then shall we go?"

"I'm ready if you are."

He motioned to Sunny for the bill, and when it came, Monique argued with him about who should pay. He won the battle. Even as they walked out of the café, he was aware of the curious stares that followed after them.

It was a relief to step out into the evening air. "Are we on for tomorrow?" she asked once they were back in his car. "I have the same work schedule as today, so I could be ready to go around two thirty or so."

"That works for me," he said despite his reluctance to continue on this crazy quest. She was so certain she had cleared both the mayor and the judge. But either one of them could have her mother's book locked away in a drawer at their office or in some other place.

The last thing he wanted to do was bring this up to her. He was afraid she would take even more chances with her life. He still believed that Mystique had been killed by somebody who was fairly prominent in the town. He was hoping that law enforcement would identify that person quickly, before Monique got herself into any real trouble.

They were quiet on the ride home. It wasn't a strained silence but rather a comfortable one. The grief that had momentarily gripped him during dinner was gone, stuffed away deep inside him once again.

He reached the edge of the swamp and parked his car and together they walked in. He followed her up the short bridge to her front door. She unlocked it and then turned back to him.

Twilight colors painted her features in a soft, golden light. For just a minute, his fingers itched to run through the silky-looking strands of her hair. He wanted to stroke her cheek to feel the softness of her skin.

Damn, what the hell was wrong with him? He took a step back from her and frowned. "I guess I'll see you tomorrow," he said and then quickly turned on his heels and headed deeper into the swamp to his shanty.

He definitely needed to keep more distance between himself and Monique as they continued her hunt. There

was something about her that reminded him of all he
had lost.

There was definitely something about her that reminded him he was a healthy, virile man who had been
without a woman for a very long time. Would he be this
attracted to just any woman who came into his world?

He didn't think so. It was specific to Monique with
her big brown eyes and luxurious hair. It was specific
to her because of her warm, beautiful smiles and her in-
sistence that he smile.

Dammit, he should have never agreed to help her.
His job was to keep her out of trouble, but he had a feeling, if he wasn't careful, he was going to get himself in
trouble with her.

Chapter Four

"Spill it, girl," Angelique said to Monique, a week later.

"Yeah, we want to know everything that's going on between you and the mysterious Jacque LeBlanc," Dominique added.

The three sisters were having breakfast at the café, something they tried to do whenever possible considering their varied work schedules. They had already ordered and now were waiting for their meals to arrive.

For the last week, Monique and Jacque had continued their search for her mother's book, working down the list of potential suspects they had made.

"There's not a lot to tell," she replied. "I'm sure by now you've heard about Jacque's reading program in the swamp. When I bumped into him one day, he told me all about it, and I offered to help introduce him to people who could help."

She hated to lie to her sisters, but if she told them the truth of what they were doing, then both of them would jump down her throat. Besides, it was important to keep what they were doing a secret.

"What's he like?" Dominique asked.

Monique frowned thoughtfully. "He's intense and at times a bit brooding and brusque. But it's strange… I sense a real kindness in him. I've spent several hours a day for a little over a week with him, and I still feel like I don't know him at all. Despite that, I like him."

However, for some reason she wanted to get to know him better. He intrigued her. She sensed there was a softness, a vulnerability deep inside him, and she wanted to unpeel all the layers he had.

She hadn't felt this kind of interest in a man since she'd dated Brody Beador for a year. Brody, a fisherman in the swamp, was the only man she'd ever slept with, and she'd believed he was her person. But when he'd gone to work on a big fishing boat for two months, she quickly learned that distance didn't make the heart grow fonder. Eventually, the two broke up. That had been two years ago.

"We heard you had dinner with him at the café," Angelique said, pulling Monique back to the conversation. "That certainly sounds a little deeper than just getting donations for a reading program."

Monique laughed. "Trust me, that dinner meant nothing. We were just out getting donations, and we got hungry."

"Well, you two are certainly all the gossip around town," Dominique said. "Everyone's shocked to see the mystery man out and about and in your company."

They paused the conversation as the waitress arrived with their breakfasts. Angelique had ordered pancakes, Dominique had opted for French toast, and Monique had gotten a cheese-and-bacon omelet.

"Thanks, Glenda," Dominique said to the older waitress.

"Just let me know if you need anything else," Glenda replied with a smile.

"Do you know where Jacque is from?" Angelique asked the moment they were alone again.

"Baton Rouge," Monique replied. "He moved to the swamp about four years ago."

"What did he do in Baton Rouge? What was his job?" Dominique asked as she cut into her French toast.

"He's never said, and I haven't asked him," Monique replied.

"Don't you think that's important to know?" Dominique asked.

"Not really. I don't care about where he worked in the past," Monique replied even as she admitted to herself she'd like to know everything about him.

She was relieved when they all began to eat and the conversation turned to the upcoming fall festival.

It was a day of celebration that took place on Main Street. A bandstand was set up in front of City Hall, and the businesses all held sidewalk sales. A local band provided music, and along with the café, other people set out fun specialty food to sell. Local artists also sold their wares.

"Are you planning to have a sidewalk sale?" Monique asked Angelique. Angelique now owned a business. Mystique's Magic sold not only luxury bath products but also ointments and medicines made of swamp plants and flowers. The store was a tribute to their mother. As always, thoughts of her mother brought up an aching grief inside her. Monique was more determined than ever to somehow find her mother's book and identify the killer.

"I'm definitely planning on having a sidewalk sale," Angelique replied. "In fact, I've already made a list of things I'll be selling at special prices that day."

"What about you, Monique? How are things going with your work?" Dominique asked.

"Very well. In fact, Debbie told me she's coming in around ten today to have an important chat with me," Monique replied, referring to Debbie Waltrip, the owner of All That Jazz. "I'm pretty sure she wants to offer me the manager job."

"That would mean a lot more responsibility on your shoulders. Are you sure you can handle it?" Angelique asked.

"Of course I can," Monique replied, grateful that she betrayed none of the irritation she felt that her sister would even question her capabilities. How surprised they'd both be when she ended up being the one who brought down their mother's killer, she thought.

"Then congrats are in order," Dominique said.

"It's a bit too soon for congratulations," Monique replied. "She might be coming in to offer me the job of wearing a clown suit for the fall festival."

Both Angelique and Dominique laughed. They finished eating, with her sisters talking about how happy they were in their relationships.

"Being with Daniel makes me feel complete," Angelique said.

"You were pretty complete without him," Monique replied dryly.

"Oh, you know what I mean," Angelique replied. "Don't you want to find your one true love?"

"Someday," Monique replied. "But I'm not in any hurry. I need the murder solved before I can even think about love."

"We all need the murder solved. I know how hard

Daniel and Luke are working on it, but it's difficult without any clues to follow," Angelique said.

Monique looked at her watch. "I hate to do this, but I've got to run. My shift at the store starts at nine." She withdrew a twenty from her purse and handed it to Angelique. "That should cover my breakfast. I'll talk to you two later."

After a round of goodbyes, Monique got up and left the café. It was another hot day with the sun a bright yellow orb in the perfect blue sky.

Pulling around the back of the dress shop to park, she reflected on how she did love her job as an assistant manager. Still, she was hungry for the possibility of becoming the manager with hiring and firing powers, along with the ability to order the fashion they sold.

As Monique entered through the back door, the pleasant scents of lilac and vanilla greeted her. She had learned that women tended to buy more if the place where they shopped smelled attractive. She made sure there were always scented plug-ins all around the store.

She turned on all the lights and then went to the front door to unlock it and flip the sign in the window to Open. She stored her purse on a shelf beneath the register counter and then grabbed some window cleaner and a cloth and wiped down the top of the display table where the register sat. When she was finished with that, she moved to the display tables to make sure everything was arranged properly.

The shop was quite colorful. Clothing hung from the racks around the walls, and a table held a variety of shoes and purses. Another table held scarves and costume jewelry all artfully arranged by her. Debbie was retirement age, and over the last few months she'd begun stepping away from the day-to-day operations.

The store did very little business when it first opened each morning, and today was no different. At ten o'clock, Debbie walked in. She was a stylish older woman with salt-and-pepper hair cut in a short bob. She was a good, fair boss, and Monique had mad respect for her.

"Hi, Monique," she greeted as she slowly walked over to where Monique had just returned to the counter.

"Hi, Debbie. I see you're wearing one of our most popular brands today, and you look fabulous," Monique replied.

Debbie was clad in a long navy skirt with pink flowers and a ruffled navy blouse. A pink scarf was around her neck, giving her a youthful flair. She smiled. "Thank you, and might I say the same about you. I've always liked the fact that you often wear our brands in your personal life. You're a walking advertisement for us."

Monique laughed. "My sisters tell me I spend way too much of my paycheck in here."

"Like that's a bad thing," Debbie replied with a laugh. "So the reason I wanted to speak with you this morning is because my rheumatoid arthritis is getting worse… much worse."

"Oh, Debbie, I'm so sorry," Monique replied. She had noticed the twisted condition of Debbie's hands, but hadn't asked what the condition was. Although she had assumed it was some kind of arthritis.

"Ah, you play with the cards you're dealt, right? Anyway, it's making it more and more difficult for me to get around. There is nobody I trust more than you when it comes to this store. You're not only my top seller, but you're hardworking and honest as the day is long."

"Thank you," Monique replied.

"So I'm sure you know why I'm here. I want you to be my full-time manager, Monique." For the next few minutes Debbie detailed what the job would entail. "So are you interested in the position?" she finished.

"Debbie, I would be honored to be your manager," Monique replied.

"Wonderful," Debbie replied. "Since I've already set the work schedules for this week, and I just ordered some new items, why don't we say starting next week you're in charge of all of it?"

"It's a job I won't take lightly," Monique replied.

Debbie smiled once again. "I know that, and I can rest easy knowing you're in charge here."

At that moment the little bell above the door tinkled as two women came in. "I'm out of here," Debbie said. "We'll talk again soon."

She walked out the door, and Monique went to help the two women.

Monique was working a full day today and wouldn't get off until five, so she and Jacque had decided they wouldn't go out tonight. She told herself she was disappointed not to be continuing on her quest, but the truth was, she was also more than a little disappointed that she wouldn't be seeing Jacque.

The more time she spent with him, the more she was attracted to him. It was not only an emotional attraction but a strong physical one as well. His big body was perfectly proportioned. Broad shoulders tapered to a slim waist and long legs. She definitely felt more than a small burn of physical attraction for him...not that anything would come of it.

The searches so far had been a bit disappointing. So many of the houses had two stories and there was no way she could go upstairs to search. She needed to figure out a way to get people to invite her into their bedrooms, but so far, no viable ideas had struck her.

The business in the dress shop that day was fairly steady, making the hours go by quickly. At five o'clock, Cynthia came in to work until close.

Monique left the shop and got into her car to go home. She was excited about her promotion to manager. She loved the store as if it belonged to her, and she was really going to enjoy being the buyer for it. There was a lot of responsibility that went with the title, but she was definitely up for it all.

Funny, the person she most wanted to tell about her promotion was Jacque. Maybe she'd even be able to coax a smile out of him.

As far as her sisters were concerned, they had always doubted her abilities and thought of her as weak and ineffectual. Being the baby of the family definitely carried a burden with it. She was eager to prove them both wrong by catching the killer who had eluded everyone else. Then they would have to accept that she was as strong and smart as they were.

She parked in the lot in front of the swamp, her thoughts on what she was going to make for dinner. While she had a variety of meat in her cooler, most of it would take too long to cook. However, she had a small bag of scallops that was calling her name. Frying them up and adding a salad would be good and quick. She walked quickly to her place, eager to get in her pajamas and relax for the rest of the evening.

When she reached her shanty, there was a sheet of paper taped to her front door. She stopped at the foot of her bridge and stared at it. From this vantage point, she couldn't see what it said, but the fact that it was there alarmed her.

Both of her sisters in the recent past had received threatening notes on their doors. Angelique's had warned of something bad about to happen now that their voodoo mother was dead. Dominique's had been from the obsessed man who had eventually kidnapped her.

Who had left her a note and why? It didn't have to be anything bad, she told herself, but that didn't staunch the small chill that slithered up her spine. In any case, she wouldn't know what it was until she read it.

On leaden feet, she walked slowly up the bridge and reached the door. She tore the note off and read it.

STOP WHAT YOU'RE DOING

The words were written in bright red ink, and there was a skull and crossbones drawn at the bottom of the page.

She shot a quick look around but saw nobody. She unlocked the door and quickly went inside. On trembling legs, she walked to the sofa and collapsed, fear still racing through her. She dropped the chilling note on the coffee table in front of her and stared at it.

STOP WHAT YOU'RE DOING

Had somebody figured out what she and Jacque were up to? That was the only thing the note could be about.

Who had left it? A new chill raced through her as she realized the very real possibility that her mother's killer had written it.

JACQUE ATTACKED THE bushes and vines creeping too close to his house with a machete. Sweat rolled down his shoulders and pooled in the center of his back as insects buzzed in the humid air.

It was always a battle keeping the swamp away from the exterior of his shanty. Keeping the area around it cleared out assured that no unwelcomed critters would find their way inside.

He was just about finished when he started to grab a vine and then froze. About a foot in front of him a large snake coiled around the thick vine. It was not just any snake. It was a northern cottonmouth, one of the venomous snakes the swamp housed.

It had a blunt snout and elliptical eyes. Jacque knew from his reading that it also had heat sensing pits between the eyes and nostrils.

The snake would now be sizing him up, trying to discern if he would be aa threat. Jacque remained frozen, his muscles tensed. The last thing he wanted was to startle it enough that it lashed out. After several stressful minutes, the snake finally slithered away. Jacque released a deep sigh of relief and decided to call it a day.

He went inside, grabbed a towel and then headed for the shower.

Minutes later he toweled off and headed back into the shanty.

He looked forward to a quiet evening. He wasn't upset about not going out with Monique tonight. Each time they went out, he was filled with tension and worried that danger could come at any moment.

But that wasn't all that bothered him about spending time with Monique.

She'd awakened a hunger in him…the hunger a man felt for a woman. He hadn't believed he would ever feel a physical attraction for a woman again. He'd been dead wrong. He tried to tell himself that he would have felt that way about any woman he spent any amount of time with, but he'd be lying to himself.

It was Monique herself. Monique with her full breasts and small waist. Even though she was short and petite, she had an hourglass figure he found very attractive. Whenever they were together, her full lips seemed to beckon him for a kiss.

But no matter what, he wouldn't act on his attraction to her. He'd sworn to himself he'd never care about anyone again.

Already, he liked her. He liked that there was a softness about her. Although he didn't agree with her plan, he liked the fact that she was passionate about it. He admired how she handled herself with other people. There was a grace about her he found quite appealing.

He consciously shoved all these thoughts away as he dressed in a pair of clean jeans and a navy T-shirt and then headed back into the living room where he sank down in his recliner and picked up the book he'd been reading.

Most evenings he either went out to do a little fishing or he read. He was partial to thrillers along with an occasional fantasy or dystopic read. He felt sorry for the souls who either didn't know how or who chose not to read. He enjoyed the escapism it granted him and how he always seemed to learn something new.

As far as he was concerned, reading anything heightened intelligence and opened up a world of new ideas. That was why he was so committed to the men in the swamp who wanted to learn to read.

He was soon engrossed in the book. However, it wasn't long before a knock fell on his door. Who the hell could it be? Other than the men he taught, nobody ever came to his door in the evenings. He got up and went to answer.

"Monique," he said in surprise at the sight of her. As always, she looked lovely in a pair of jeans and a bright red fitted blouse. What wasn't lovely was the deep frown she wore.

"I'm sorry. Am I confused? Were we supposed to go out tonight?" he asked.

"No, but something has happened. Can I come in?" Her dark eyes radiated concern, along with a touch of excitement. Definitely a strange combination. She grasped a piece of paper in her hand.

"Come on in," he replied. As she swept past him, he caught a whiff of her perfume…the scent he found so attractive. He gestured her to the sofa, wondering why she was here. "Uh…would you like something to drink?" he asked.

"No, I'm fine, but I need you to see something. When I got home from work today, this was taped to my front door." She handed him the piece of paper.

STOP WHAT YOU'RE DOING

The letters seemed to jump off the page, along with the skull and crossbones drawn at the bottom. His chest muscles tightened, and he looked back up at her.

"It's got to be from my mother's killer, right?" she said.

He sank down in his recliner and gazed once again at the note. "It very well could be," he replied. He looked back at her. "It's obvious somebody has somehow figured out we aren't just asking for book donations. We need to stop our snooping right now. This note is definitely a warning."

"No, Jacque," she exclaimed as she leaned slightly forward. "Don't you see? We've got somebody worried. Now isn't the time to stop."

He waved the note in the air. "This doesn't frighten you?"

Her cheeks filled with color, and she drew in several deep breaths. "Yes, it scares me, but it also gives me a lot of hope. We've made the killer nervous, and that's a good thing, right? Now more than ever we need to keep pushing forward. A nervous killer might make a mistake, right?"

"Monique, be reasonable. If that is truly from your mother's killer, then you're in his sights. If we don't stop, the killer might very well come after you." His stomach clenched at the very thought of her coming to any harm.

He got up and set the note on his coffee table, then returned to his recliner. "I'd sure like to know how somebody saw through our ruse. Did you tell anyone about what we were really doing? Anyone at all? Maybe one of your sisters?"

"No, I haven't told a soul," she said. "What about you?"

"I don't have a soul to tell, so no, I haven't told anyone."

She frowned. "Maybe since the killer stole the client book, us asking for donations of books hits too close to home for him. That's possible, isn't it?" Her gaze held his intently, as if she needed to know his most inner thoughts.

"Hell, Monique. At this point anything is possible." He released a sigh of deep frustration. Something like this was the last thing he'd expected and exactly what he was worried about. "I still think it's time we stop what we're doing. You aren't getting the full results anyway with all the two-story houses."

She flushed once again. "But I'm getting some houses cleared. For the next week, why don't we just focus on the people who live in one-story homes? At least in them I can check out all the drawers in the main bedroom."

"Are you not hearing me?" He could admire her determination but not in this case. His frustration with her was nearly overwhelming. "You are a stubborn little… uh…woman." This time he leaned forward in his chair, his voice brusque. "You are now on notice that you could be in real danger. You would be a damned fool to follow on the same path."

"Then call me a damned fool," she replied tersely.

"What you need to do is take this note to Daniel and confess to him what we've been doing. Let the police handle it from here."

"Maybe that's what I should do, but I'm not going to do it," she replied, her chin lifted with defiance. Her dark eyes sparkled with a sharp boldness. "I'm going to continue this, and hopefully the nervous killer will make a mistake that will get him arrested."

"Or you dead," he muttered.

"I'm not about to let anyone get close enough to kill me," she said. "And I'm not about to do what some anonymous note tells me to do, either. Jacque, I intend to go forward with or without your help, and if you go to Daniel with all this, I'll never, ever forgive you and even that won't stop me from continuing."

He sighed and raked a hand through his hair in frustration. "There's no way in hell I'm going to let you do this on your own, so I guess count me in." He wasn't happy about this. He wasn't happy about it at all.

She smiled then…that beautiful smile that lit him up inside. "Thank you, Jacque."

"Don't thank me," he half growled. "And don't smile at me. I'm making my decision under extreme duress. I don't want you out there all alone with no backup. Things need to be different from now on. Do you own a gun?"

"No." The smile quickly fell from her face.

"Monique, if you really intend to follow through with all this, then you need to watch your surroundings. I would prefer that you not be out alone, and when you are out you need to carry a weapon."

"I have a wicked knife I could start carrying," she said soberly. Her eyes widened slightly. "Do you really think the killer would go so far as to come after me?"

"Absolutely, especially if he feels threatened by you. He's already a cold-blooded murderer. What's one more dead woman if that keeps him safe from discovery? He obviously already feels threatened enough to leave you an ominous note. Monique, this is nothing to take lightly."

"I'll just have to be more aware of who gets close to me and make sure when I am out that it's in a public place." she said. "Trust me, Jacque, I'm no fool." A steely strength shone from her long-lashed eyes. She suddenly stood. "Now, I've bothered you long enough for one night. I think it's time for me to head home."

He rose from the recliner. "I'll walk you home."

"Do you really think that's necessary? I don't want to be a bother."

"We can't know from what direction the danger might come. Just wait there for one minute." He hurried into his bedroom and grabbed his gun and holster. Once they were on, he returned to the living room.

She obviously saw his gun and gazed up at him. "But I thought we'd figured out that the killer is somebody in town."

"We might be wrong about that. Besides anybody from town could easily walk into the swamp to come after you." He walked with her to the front door, and together they stepped outside.

Twilight had fallen, painting the surroundings in a deep purple light. Thick shadows danced around the base of the trees, along with a humid mist that swirled in the air.

As they walked, he stayed close to her side, his gaze shooting all around. They didn't speak, so the only sounds were bullfrogs croaking and occasional rustling in the bushes they passed.

He walked with her up the bridge to her front door. She unlocked it and then turned back to him. She wore the colors of twilight well, and he thought he'd never seen her look prettier.

"I work until three tomorrow, so I can be ready to go by around three thirty," she said. She surprised him by reaching out and taking his hand in hers. She smiled up at him. "I guess we had our first fight tonight. I know you aren't happy with the outcome, but I appreciate you." She squeezed his hand and then released it.

He was filled with a sudden sharp desire to take her into his arms and kiss her lush lips. An electricity snapped in the air…sizzling all through his veins. He leaned slightly toward her.

Her eyes widened a bit, and her lips parted as if in open invitation.

What the hell was he doing? He snapped himself upright and took a step back from her. "Then I'll just see you tomorrow. Good night, Monique."

"Good night, Jacque."

He waited until she was safely in the shanty, and only then did he turn to head back to his.

He was still trying to process everything that had happened. The note scared him for her. Who had left it? How on earth had anyone found out what they were doing? One thing was for sure, he definitely found her stubbornness absolutely maddening. It had been one thing to indulge her in her desire to find her mother's book, but now the note brought a new layer of danger to the whole thing.

He reached his shanty and went inside. He collapsed back in his recliner.

He couldn't believe how badly he'd wanted to kiss her.

She had full, luscious lips that appeared to beg for a kiss. But kissing her would only make his situation worse.

The last thing he wanted to do was deepen how much he cared for Monique. It was bad enough that he cared about her at all. One thing he had learned in life was the absolute hell that occurred when you lost somebody you loved.

He might not love Monique, but he'd definitely grown to care about her, and that scared him. Because of her desire to ignore danger and continue on her path, he would do everything in his power to keep her safe.

Then, when this was all over, he'd go back to being the loner he intended to be.

Chapter Five

"That color looks absolutely gorgeous on you, and the fit is perfect," Monique said to Nicole Adderman, a young woman who was a frequent shopper. She was trying on a deep emerald-colored blouse that looked terrific against her pale blond hair.

Nicole looked at herself in the mirror on the outside of the fitting room door. "It does look nice, doesn't it?" She turned and smiled at Monique. "I'll take it."

Minutes later Monique was once again alone in the shop. She glanced up at the clock on the wall. She was working until close tonight, and she had three more hours to go.

For the last week, she and Jacque had been out doing their thing. They'd focused on prominent people who lived in one-story homes. Jacque now had a back seat full of donated books, but the one book they sought remained elusive.

Jacque continued to be an enigma. At times brusque and withdrawn and at other times a bit more open, there was just something about him that continued to draw her to him. Aside from her simmering physical attraction to him, she sensed a deep pain inside him, one she wanted to root out and soothe. It was odd, really. His silences drew her closer to him, and his brusqueness she met with a soft voice and an attempt to coax out one of his stingy smiles.

The bell tinkled over the door, and Nola walked in. "You used to stop by my house pretty regularly for a little girl chat. Now I have to come chase you down at work if I want to see you."

Monique grinned. "I do miss our girl talks, Nola. So are you here to chat or to shop?"

"Definitely to chat. I'm out of money right now, so I'm not doing any shopping," Nola replied.

"Do you need to borrow some money?" Monique asked in concern. Nola had been a constant since childhood. She was the favorite aunt who always had candy in her purse and a warm hug for all the Santori girls. If she needed a little cash to tide her over, Monique would be more than happy to help her. Nola had never married and had always considered Mystique and her girls, her family.

"Oh no, I'll be just fine. I just need to watch my pennies right now. Besides, I hope to sell a lot of things at the fall festival next week, and hopefully that will put me right as rain."

Nola painted on small logs and fallen bark and rocks, creating beautiful works of art. She sold many of them online and had recently worked out a deal with Angelique to sell some of her creations at Mystique's Magic.

"Now, I know what's going on in Angelique and Dominique's lives, but you and I haven't touched base recently. You've always been the quieter one, but I know still water runs deep, so tell me what's been going on with you," Nola said.

"You're now looking at the new manager of All That Jazz," Monique said with pride.

"Oh, honey, that's wonderful. I know how much you wanted it." Nola reached out and pulled her into a big hug. It felt familiar and almost as good as being hugged by her mother. "Your mother would be so proud of you."

"Thanks," Monique replied, thankful that the words hadn't pulled forth the ever-present sorrow that could engulf her at any time.

"Now, tell me what's going on between you and the very handsome Jacque," Nola went on. "You're spending quite a lot of time with him. I would think by now he has enough donated books to start a library."

Monique laughed. "We are getting a lot of donations, but there are a lot of men and women in the swamp eager to participate in the literacy program."

"It's an admirable thing he's doing," Nola said.

"Yes, it is."

"You like him," Nola replied with a gleam in her eyes.

"Oh, Nola, I do like him very much, and I don't know why," Monique confessed. "I still don't know a lot about him, but he just draws me in."

"Just be careful with your heart, honey," Nola said. "Don't rush things and don't give your heart away until you're very sure of what you're doing."

"Don't worry about that. I'm in no danger of giving my heart away any time soon," Monique said with a laugh. "I just like him, that's all." She wasn't about to share with Nola her desire for Jacque to take her in his arms and kiss her until she was mindless with passion.

The two women visited for a few minutes longer, and then the conversation halted when a couple of shoppers came in. Nola said a quick goodbye and left while Monique tended to the customers.

It was nearing closing time when Jackson Scott, the district attorney, came into the shop. It wasn't that unusual for the tall, good-looking middle-aged bachelor to come in to buy something for his latest honey.

"Ah, Monique, my dear," he greeted her with a wide smile. "I'm so glad you're the one working. You always steer me in the right direction when I'm buying something."

"Thank you, Mr. Scott. I'm always happy to help you." She kept a pleasant smile on her face even though she'd always found the DA to be rather slimy.

While he was handsome with blond hair, brilliant blue eyes and chiseled features, he thought he was all that and a bag of chips. However, Monique knew that in truth he was a serial dater who initially love-bombed the women he took out and then quickly cooled off and moved on to another woman, leaving broken hearts in his wake.

"I'm looking for something nice for Ali Sanders. Do you know her?"

"I'm sorry, but I don't think I do," Monique replied.

"She works at the laundromat and is a sweet, very attractive blonde. We've just started dating, so I don't want to spend too much money, but I want to get her something nice," he explained.

"How about a pretty silk scarf?" Monique suggested. "We have some really nice ones here, and I think any woman would like one."

"That might work," he replied and followed Monique to the table where the scarves were displayed.

As he picked through them, Monique suddenly realized that darkness had fallen outside, and she was alone with one of the men who was on her suspect list.

It gave her some comfort that on the shelf next to her purse at the register, her knife was open and ready to use. The knife was sharp enough to gut a man if necessary, although she hoped it would never come to that.

"This is pretty," he said as he picked up a hot pink and bright yellow one. "Yeah, I'll take it. Could you wrap it up real nice?"

"Of course," she replied.

"Aside from working here, what have you been up to lately?" he asked.

"I've been helping Jacque LeBlanc." As she wrapped the scarf box with pretty pink paper, she explained about getting donations of books for the people in the swamp.

"Yeah, I heard something about that. Feel free to come to my place, I'm sure I have some books I could donate," he said.

"Thanks, we'll do that."

Minutes later he was gone, and it was time for her to close up the shop and head home. She locked the door and turned off all the lights except one spotlight that shone down on the register.

She counted the cash and added up the card transactions and then compared everything with the sales for the day. Satisfied that the numbers all matched, she wrote out a bank deposit slip. She would drive through the bank and make the deposit on her way home.

As she finished up, her thoughts went back to Jackson Scott. In the next day or two, she and Jacque would be visiting with the man to talk about Jacque's program and give her a chance to search for her mother's book in his home.

She was aware that her plan to catch the killer had flaws. Two-story homes were impossible to search. There was also the possibility that the book wasn't even in a drawer at all.

However, she was hoping and praying that somehow, someway, she'd stumble on the book in one of the places they were searching and the murderer would be unmasked. She needed that to happen so badly. She desperately needed the closure.

She finally turned off the last light and then headed for the back exit, her knife gripped firmly in her hand. Her car was parked just outside the back door.

It was only after she was in the vehicle with all the doors locked that she set the knife down in the passenger seat next to her purse. She was taking her safety very seriously since receiving the note on her door.

The night was unusually dark with just a sliver of the moon visible. A layer of thick fog added to the lack of visibility, slowing her drive to the swamp.

She yawned and fought against a wave of exhaustion. It had been a long day, and she was looking forward to getting home and going to bed.

Tomorrow she was on duty to open the store and work until two, and then she and Jacque would continue their work. She always looked forward to spending more time with him. Each time they were together, she tried to find the key that would make him really open up to her.

She finally reached the swamp entrance and parked. She got out of the car with her knife once again gripped tightly in her hand. She walked briskly, listening to make sure nobody was on the path with her.

A few minutes later she breathed a sigh of relief as she reached her shanty door. Once inside, she turned on a few of the lanterns in the living room and then carried one into the bedroom. She placed the knife on her nightstand and then took off the clothes she'd worn to work and hung them in her closet.

She pulled on a hot pink nightshirt and then returned to the living room. She was a bit hungry but didn't want to cook. But she hadn't eaten all day and knew she wanted something. She finally settled for some crackers and cheese. She sat on the sofa to eat them, and as she did, her thoughts went over the past week.

She and Jacque had cleared another five houses without incident. There were only three names left on their list, although she'd already thought of a couple more to add.

Was she adding names to the list so she could continue to see Jacque? She knew once she quit going to homes the odds were good that she would never see him again except in passing.

She wasn't sure of the answer and in any case, she was too tired to think anymore. She finished eating and then returned the leftover crackers to the kitchen.

Finally, she turned off all the lanterns except the one she'd carried back into her bedroom. Once she was settled in bed, she turned that one off. Other than a faint illumination that drifted through her window, the room was plunged in darkness. The sound of croaking frogs competed with the faint sound of insects, creating a lullaby she heard every night. It was familiar and soothing, and she fell asleep almost immediately.

She was awakened a bit later by a hard knock on her front door. She glanced at her phone on the nightstand next to her. Ten thirty. It was possible it might be one of her sisters, but she doubted it. They never came by this late, and they would have called first.

She grabbed her knife from her nightstand, turned on the lantern and carried it into the living room. She lit several more lanterns, and then gripping the knife firmly in her hand, she called out to ask who it was.

Not receiving an answer but still curious, she eased open her front door.

Nobody was there. She looked around but didn't see anyone. She was about to close her door when she saw a small box on her porch. It was the size of a jewelry box. She looked around once again and then bent down to pick it up.

Out of her peripheral vision, she saw a dark shape rushing toward her.

The person, all in black and wearing a mask, slammed into her body with enough force to knock her off the porch and to the ground. Before she could get up, the person kicked her. Again and again, the kicks hit her in her ribs, forcing the breath out of her as pain racked her body.

In an effort to protect herself, she curled up in a fetal position as sobs escaped her. She'd dropped her knife when the attacker rammed into her, and now she had nothing to use for her own protection.

She tried to scream, but the sounds that left her were more like kitten mewls. She didn't have enough air in her lungs to really scream and her ribs were on fire.

She needed to get up. Somehow, she needed to stand up and fight back, but the constant kicks to her body made it impossible for her to rise.

Finally, the kicks stopped. Before she could catch her breath, the attacker began pummeling her around the head. One particular blow landed on the side of her chin, and stars momentarily danced in her head.

If she didn't do something, she feared she would be beaten to death. Despite the agonizing pain that torched through her, in spite of being hit over and over again, she began to crawl toward the porch. Inch by painful inch, she crawled. Hopefully the attacker hadn't seen her knife. And hopefully she could find it and use it to halt the beating once and for all.

She summoned up the strength and screamed once again, this time with enough force that birds squawked and flew from their nighttime perches.

"Monique…is that you?" Bill Stanger, the busboy at the café and her nearest neighbor, yelled out from his front porch.

"Bill…help me!" she cried.

Her assailant delivered one final kick, and then Monique heard him running away.

Thankfully Bill came to help her. He took one look at her and then gently scooped her up in his arms and carried her inside and to her sofa as she cried with intense pain.

"Where's your phone, Monique? I need to call the police, and you need an ambulance. Where's your phone?" he asked again urgently.

"On my…my nightstand," she managed to gasp out.

It didn't take long before Daniel and a team of his men

entered her shanty. Daniel rushed to her side. "Monique, are you okay? Can you tell me what happened?"

She spoke haltingly amid her tears, explaining what had happened from the time she received the knock on her door until Bill came to help her. He only asked her a few questions about the physical description of the attacker, which she couldn't answer, and then the medical team came in with a stretcher to take her to the hospital.

"Daniel, can you do me one favor?" she asked amid tears. "Would you call Jacque and tell him what's happened?"

"I'll be glad to do that," he replied.

As they carried her outside, she continued to weep with pain and fear. The only person she wanted with her right now was her partner in crime, the man who she knew would make her feel safe.

It was just after eleven thirty when Jacque's phone rang. He saw that it was Daniel, and sleep immediately fell away.

"Chief, what's going on?" he asked.

"Monique has been attacked," Daniel replied.

Jacque shot up in the bed. "Where?"

"In front of her shanty. I don't know exactly what happened, but she asked that I call you."

"Where is she now?" Jacque asked as he quickly scrambled out of bed.

"I had her taken to the hospital. She should be there now."

"Thanks." Jacque hung up and immediately got dressed. He grabbed his phone and his car keys and quickly left his shanty.

His thoughts were in turmoil as he hurried through the swamp to get to his car. Daniel had said she'd been attacked. What exactly did that mean and how badly had she been hurt?

Damn, he should have asked more questions. Hopefully he'd get answers when he reached the hospital. What had she been doing outside her shanty at this time of night? He should have insisted she stop with her snooping after she'd received the threatening note. If this attack was about that, then she was done. He would make damned sure of it.

He reached his car and roared off toward the small hospital that served the town.

His gut tightened in knots of tension, and anger battled with anxiety inside him. The anger was mostly directed at himself for indulging her in the hunt for her mother's elusive book. He should have never agreed to any of it in the first place. What he should have done was go to Daniel and let the lawman know her intentions. Right now, he couldn't figure out exactly why he hadn't done that.

It didn't take long for him to pull into the parking lot in front of the emergency room entrance. Jumping out of the car, he raced inside and approached the woman at the receptionist desk. "I'm here for Monique Santori," he said.

"She's back with the doctor right now. If you'll just take a seat, somebody will be out to talk to you when they can," she said.

"Thanks," he replied, then sank down in one of the green plastic chairs against a wall.

Would he even be allowed to speak to anyone about her condition? He wasn't related to her in any way. With all the privacy laws, he had no idea. But she had wanted him to know what happened. She had asked Daniel to call him.

She had been attacked. That was all he really knew. Had she been stabbed? Shot? How, exactly, had she been attacked? The fact that she'd needed to come to the hospital ripped him up inside.

He was the only person in the waiting room, and as he sat alone with his thoughts, he couldn't help but be wildly worried about her.

It was about thirty minutes later when Daniel came in. "Any news?" he asked as he sat down in the chair next to Jacque.

"Not yet," Jacque replied. "Can you tell me exactly what happened?"

"Somebody tried to beat the hell out of her."

All of Jacque's muscles tightened once again, and he felt sick to his stomach. She had been beaten? "How bad?"

Daniel frowned. "Hard to tell. According to her, most of the blows were to her body. You have any idea who might have done this to her?"

"None. What the hell was she doing outside her shanty at that time of night? Did she say?" Jacque asked.

"Yeah, she said somebody knocked on her door. When she went to answer nobody was there, but there was a small box on her porch. She bent down to pick it up, and that's when somebody in dark clothes and a ski mask slammed into her hard enough to knock her off the porch and to the ground."

"Do her sisters know about this?"

"I haven't told them yet. Angelique knew I got an

emergency call, but she didn't know it was at Monique's shanty. I wanted to sort through all the details before telling them." Daniel shifted in the chair. "I found the box she talked about at the scene, and I opened it. I figured it was probably empty, but there was a note inside. It said *I warned you*. Do you know what that's all about?"

Jacque was torn between the need to tell Daniel the truth and Monique's desire to keep it a secret. "You'll have to ask Monique about that," he finally said. "Was she able to give you any kind of a description of the person who attacked her?"

"No, as I said before, the person was dressed all in black and wore a mask. Monique said everything happened so fast she had no idea as to height or weight."

"It's too bad she couldn't give you something to go on," Jacque replied, his stomach still aching for her.

"Yeah, that seems to be the story of my cases right now," Daniel replied with obvious frustration.

At that moment Dr. Gregory Harmon walked out to greet them. Jacque had seen the older doctor a couple of times in the past four years for a variety of ailments, so he knew who he was.

Both Jacque and Daniel stood as he approached them. "She's going to be okay," Dr. Harmon said. "Although in the next couple of days and weeks, she's going to hurt." He looked from Jacque to Daniel. "She has two fractured ribs and various bruises. I had every intention of keeping her here for the rest of the night, but she insists she wants to go home. She should be out here in just a few minutes. I've given her a week's worth of pain meds. Unfortunately, there isn't much that can be done for cracked ribs. What she really needs is plenty of rest and to give herself time to heal"

"Thank you, Doctor," Daniel said. As Dr. Harmon left them, he commented, "I was going to question Monique a little more, but it can wait until tomorrow."

"You go ahead and take off and do whatever you need to do, I'll take Monique home," Jacque said.

"There's really nothing left to do. We searched all around the porch area and where we believed the attack took place, but we didn't find anything that might help identify the assailant. We'll take up the investigation again tomorrow morning in the light of day."

Minutes later Jacque was once again alone in the waiting room. He wasn't sure how long it was before Monique walked out.

She was wearing a bright pink nightshirt with a blue-flowered hospital gown over the top. She walked gingerly, as if every step was sheer torture. She had a blossoming bruise on the side of her chin. The minute she saw him, she burst into tears.

If any woman ever needed to be held, it was her. He tentatively pulled her into his arms, not wanting to hurt her further.

She buried her face in the front of his shirt as she continued to cry.

"Hey, hey…crying is only going to make you hurt more," he said softly.

She continued to weep for several more minutes, and then her sobs slowly subsided, but she continued to linger in his arms for a long moment. Finally, she raised her head and stepped back from him. "Oh, Jacque, it was so terrible. I thought I was going to be beaten to death."

He hated to see her tearstained face and he wanted to grab her back into his arms and hold her tight. He needed to make sure that nobody would ever hurt her again. These thoughts stirred up old, raw memories inside him that made him unsettled, but he shoved them away.

"Can you take me home?" she asked.

"That's what I intend to do," he replied. "Are you ready to go now?"

"More than ready," she said with a nod.

He grabbed one of her arms to steady her as they headed slowly to the exit. It didn't take long to get her in his car and then he headed back to the swamp.

For several minutes she didn't speak, and he remained silent, giving her space to remain quiet if that was what she needed.

"I was a fool," she finally said, weariness heavy in her tone. "I should have never answered the knock on my door. Even worse, I stepped out on my porch."

"Daniel told me the box that was on your porch contained a message," he said.

"A message? What was it?"

"It was a note that said you were warned."

She released a deep sigh. "If the beating had continued, I don't think I would have been alive to read the note."

"I hate to tell you this, but you're probably going to hurt more tomorrow than you do tonight," he said softly. He glanced over at her. She looked so small, so achingly vulnerable.

Two cracked ribs. He knew what kind of force was necessary to crack a rib. She must be in tremendous pain, but right now she was remarkably stoic. Even if the doctor had given her something at the hospital, a mere pill or shot couldn't take away all the pain.

"I'll get through it. Besides, I have some pain meds to take if I need them," she replied. "Before I know it, I'll be right as rain."

He admired her optimism, but he knew it was going to take a while before she fully recovered and didn't hurt anymore.

They arrived at the swamp parking area, where he hurried around to the passenger side to help her out.

Once again, they fell silent as they slowly walked in to her shanty. When they reached it, she paused for a moment at the foot of the bridge and looked up toward the porch.

It was dark, but lantern light came out of her windows, illuminating the porch area. After a moment's hesitation, she walked up the bridge, and he followed close behind her.

It had been long enough since the attack that the police had cleared out and apparently it was no longer a crime scene.

The front door was locked but she had a key hidden under a rock next to the porch. She told him where it was and he retrieved it and opened the door.

When they were inside the shanty, she pulled a bottle of pills out of the hospital gown pocket and set them down on the coffee table. She then sat on the sofa and released a small sigh. "Jacque, thank you so much for bringing me home."

"Don't get comfortable," he replied. "I want you to go pack a bag. You aren't staying here."

She looked at him in surprise. "Then where am I going to stay?"

He knew this was just another mistake in a trail of mistakes he'd already made with her, but as a man who cared for the safety of another human being, he had no choice.

"As long as your attacker is still out there, you'll be staying with me," he said.

Chapter Six

Pain. It pulled her from her sleep as it slammed into her. Her legs…her ribs…even her face hurt. It was like she'd been run over by a very large truck. There didn't seem to be any part of her body that didn't hurt tremendously.

She opened her eyes to morning light streaming in the window. For a split second she didn't know where she was. Then she remembered. The knock on her door… the beating. She was in Jacque's spare bedroom.

She had been in no condition last night to notice much of anything, so she slowly sat up and looked around with interest. She was in a queen-size bed flanked by two dark wood nightstands. A large dresser was against one wall, and there was a closet on the other wall.

The bedspread was a pretty turquoise and matching curtains hung at the window. It was a very nice room, but she didn't belong here. She'd been too frightened, too traumatized to protest Jacque's plan for her to stay here. In truth, last night she had wanted to be here. She'd been afraid to stay by herself after the beating she had taken.

But this morning she wanted to tell him that she needed to go back home. There was no way he should be burdened with her staying here in his home. She should be safe in her shanty as long as she didn't do anything stupid. She'd been incredibly stupid the night before.

With this thought in mind, she slowly pulled herself out of the bed. Her entire body protested the movement, and her ribs felt like they were on fire, but she couldn't stay in bed all day.

It took her nearly fifteen minutes to get dressed in a pair of jeans and a pink T-shirt. She brushed out her hair and then stepped out of the room with her toothpaste and toothbrush in hand.

As she left the bedroom, the scent of coffee wafted in the air. After brushing her teeth, she returned to the bedroom and tucked her toothbrush and paste back into her bag.

Finally, she walked out of the bedroom and headed for the kitchen area where Jacque was seated at the table with a cup of coffee before him. He immediately stood at the sight of her. "Coffee?"

"Yes, please," she replied.

"Sit, and I'll get you a cup. How do you like it?"

"With just a little bit of sugar." Gingerly she sank down in the chair opposite his.

It took him only a moment to place the cup of coffee in front of her and then return to his seat. "Thanks," she said as she wrapped her fingers around the warmth of the cup.

"How are you feeling?"

"A little rough," she admitted.

His green eyes held her gaze for a long moment. "I'm sure that's the understatement of the day."

She offered him a small smile. "Okay, I'm feeling a lot rough. I hurt where I didn't even know I had body parts."

"Have you taken a pain pill?" he asked.

"Not yet."

"Why don't I make us some breakfast and afterward you can take a pill and stretch out either on the sofa or go back to bed?" He stood. "I was just about to make me some bacon, eggs and toast. All you need to do is tell me how you like your eggs."

"You shouldn't be cooking for me. What I really need to do is gather my things and go back to my home." She took a sip of coffee as he stared at her.

"Monique, are you completely out of your mind? Somebody tried to kill you last night. There's no way you should be alone in your shanty right now. Dear God, woman, aren't you ever frightened?"

As she thought of the beating she'd taken the night before, hot tears suddenly burned at her eyes. "Yes, I'm frightened, and I don't want to be alone in my shanty, but I also don't want to be a burden to you. You shouldn't be taking care of me."

"Somebody needs to, and you aren't a burden. So how do you like your eggs?"

She swiped at her eyes. "Any way is fine."

He nodded, then turned around and pulled a two-burner cook stove from a cabinet. He plugged it in, grabbed an iron skillet and placed it atop the bigger burner. Within minutes he had bacon cooking.

The smell of it made her stomach rumble, and she realized despite all her pain, she was hungry. She watched him work in silence. Although he was a relatively big man, he moved with an efficiency and grace that was surprising. He didn't speak as he worked, and neither did she. She was content just to sit and watch him.

He was wearing a pair of jeans and a gray T-shirt that stretched taut across his broad shoulders and showed off his large biceps. He also had his shoulder holster strapped on with his gun. He was so damned attractive. If he would just smile more often.

She remembered how wonderful his big, strong arms had felt around her the night before. She had felt so safe, so incredibly protected in the tender shelter of his arms.

The beating must have addled her brains. Here she sat, hurting with every move she made, and yet she yearned to be back in Jacque's arms once again.

"How did you sleep?" she asked, breaking the silence that had prevailed until now.

"I slept okay," he replied.

He took the crispy bacon strips out of the skillet, drained the oil and then got an egg carton out of his cooler. He broke five eggs into a bowl, added a little milk and some shredded cheese and then poured the mixture into the awaiting skillet. As the scrambled eggs cooked, from the cabinet he got out a four-slice toaster and filled it with bread. It was only minutes later when he placed a plate before her and then sat at the table with his own.

"This all looks delicious," she said. "I hope you didn't go to all this trouble just because I'm here."

"I cook myself a good breakfast every morning," he replied. "What about you? Do you eat breakfast?"

"It depends on my work schedule. Oh, the store," she exclaimed with dismay. "I need to get in touch with Debbie and let her know I won't be in for a couple of days. Oh my gosh, I was supposed to open the shop this morning."

"Whatever you need to do, it can wait until after you eat. You should probably get in touch with your sisters and let them know you're okay and you'll be staying here."

She gazed at him for a long moment. "What exactly do I tell them? For how long will I be staying here?"

He held her gaze. "Until."

"Until when?"

"Until the person who attacked you is behind bars," he said.

"But that could be a long time before an arrest is made," she said in protest.

"Then you'll be here for a long time. Monique, I intend to keep you safe. I'm partially responsible for what's happened to you."

"Why are you responsible?" she asked.

"Because I was part of your plan when I knew it was a bad idea to begin with. I should have stopped you before we even got started. Now, eat up before it gets cold."

"You couldn't have stopped me," she replied. The whole scene felt surreal. A week ago, she would have never expected to be sitting in Jacque's kitchen having breakfast. She definitely hadn't foreseen having to stay in his shanty for her own safety.

And yet she wanted to be here. She'd initially thought she wanted to go home, but if she looked deep inside, she would admit that she was terribly frightened and didn't want to be alone in her shanty. In a couple of days, she would feel stronger, both physically and mentally, and then she would move back home.

The person who had attacked her had tried to kill her last night. That person had been unsuccessful. Would the assailant come at her again? It was a very good possibility.

The search for her mother's book had turned deadly, and she had no idea the identity of the monster. Even though she didn't want to be a burden to Jacque, at least for now she was grateful to be here and under his protection.

They finished eating in silence. "Where are your pain pills?" he asked when they were done.

"They're on my nightstand, but I don't need one right now." She didn't want to depend on pills to get her through this.

"You definitely need one. You've been squirming in your chair, and you moaned between bites," he replied.

"I did? Now I'm embarrassed."

"No need to be embarrassed. Monique, you need to take the pills until some of your pain subsides." He got up from the table. "Why don't you go stretch out on the sofa, and I'll be right back?"

She had just lowered herself to the edge of the sofa when he returned with a glass of water and her bottle of pills. He handed both to her. She swallowed the pill and then looked up at him.

"I appreciate that you're protecting me, but you don't have to play nurse."

"Somebody has to do it," he replied gruffly. "I'll go get you a pillow so you can rest here, unless you'd rather go back to the bedroom."

"I'd much rather stay out here with you," she replied.

"Then I'll get you a pillow. Do you need a blanket?"

"No, thanks, I'm fine."

A few minutes later, she was stretched out on the sofa with a bed pillow behind her head and the pain pill starting to work. Jacque had also brought her cell phone to her, obviously knowing she needed to make a few calls.

As he cleaned up the kitchen, she first called Angelique and then Dominique. Daniel had told both of them about the attack and that Jacque had been with her. He had also told them to give her some space to get settled in at Jacque's. If he hadn't told them that then she knew both of them would have already tried to see or contact her. Both were grateful she was staying with Jacque and happy that she was okay.

She then called Debbie and told her boss what had happened. "I should be in tomorrow for my shift," she said.

"Like hell," Jacque said as he came back into the living room and caught that part of her conversation. "You need more time to rest."

"Debbie, my keeper says I need more time to rest, so I'll get somebody to cover for me tomorrow, and then I'll be in for my shift the next day."

Jacque huffed in obvious irritation but didn't say anything more as he sat in his recliner. It only took her a couple more phone calls to get the schedule at the shop sorted out.

"Going back to work day after tomorrow is way too early," Jacque said once she was off her phone. "You're pushing yourself too hard, and the doctor said more than anything you needed to rest."

"My work doesn't require any hard labor," she replied.

"That doesn't matter. Being up on your feet, waiting on customers and unloading boxes is work and not the kind of rest the doctor wanted you to get."

"I'll be resting until I go back to work." A drowsiness swept over her, and she knew it was the result of the pill she had taken. She gazed at Jacque, who wore a deep scowl. "Are you going to be a big cranky-pants the whole time I'm here with you?" she asked groggily.

Unfortunately, she drifted off to sleep before she heard his reply.

CRANKY-PANTS. WAS THAT who he had become? A bitter man who couldn't even smile at the beautiful sleeping woman on his sofa?

The problem was Monique was a beautiful woman. Normally her light floral scent radiated from her, filling the air with the image of a field of beautiful flowers.

His stomach had been tied in knots from the moment she'd entered the kitchen. In her jeans and light pink T-shirt, she'd looked positively lovely even with the bruise that darkened one side of her chin.

Just the sight of that bruise had ticked him off. What kind of person could beat on a petite woman like her? It had been obvious that she'd been in tremendous pain as she'd eaten breakfast and yet she still had shared her beautiful smiles.

Watching her sleep was a guilty pleasure. Her skin was poreless and her eyelashes were so long they almost dusted the top of her cheeks. With her features in repose, she looked tranquil and without pain.

His hands tightened into fists as he thought of the beating she'd taken. Even though he wasn't a violent man, he'd love to have five minutes alone with her attacker.

Nobody would lay a finger on her now, he'd make damn sure of it. For as long as it took, he intended to be her shadow. She was marked for death by some unknown person, but Jacque would make sure no harm came to her.

This wouldn't end like the last time he had vowed to protect someone. It couldn't, because if it did, it would completely destroy him.

He picked up his latest crime novel from next to his chair and leaned back to read. He could hear her breathing. The faint rhythmic sound mingled with the familiar outdoor noise that drifted in through his back screen door. There was the occasional bird call coupled with the bushes rustling as small animals hurried on their way to forage for food. Occasionally the sound of a fish jumping could be heard from the nearby water. For Jacque these sounds soothed his soul.

A faint breeze drifted through the open kitchen window, making the room temperature quite pleasant. One of the first things he did in the mornings was open up all the windows in the shanty. At bedtime he would close all of them except the one in his bedroom.

Monique slept for a little over an hour. She released a small moan as her eyes fluttered open. The sound cut through him. He hated that she was in such pain.

Still, she slowly sat up and offered him a smile. "Did I snore?"

"No, but it wouldn't have mattered if you had. I probably snore as well."

"My sisters always teased me and said the minute I fell asleep I'd snore like a bullfrog, but I never knew if it was really true or not."

"Did they tease you a lot when you were growing up?" he asked.

"Constantly, but to be perfectly honest we all teased

each other." She swung her legs around so she was sitting on the sofa and gazed at him curiously. "Do you have brothers or sisters, Jacque?"

"No, I'm an only child."

"Where are your parents?"

"My father passed away five years ago from prostate cancer, and my mother passed seven years ago from a heart attack." Thank God they had both been gone before the event that had destroyed Jacque's life.

"Oh, I'm so sorry to hear that," she replied, her gaze soft and sympathetic.

"Thanks, but it was a long time ago."

"Does it get easier?" She gazed at him intently. "Because right now for me the heartache of missing my mother hasn't lessened at all. It lives inside me with such pain, and even after all these months it hasn't gotten any better."

"Time does help," he replied.

"I still feel like I won't even begin healing until her killer is caught. My life is at a standstill because I need to have the closure of him being thrown into jail." She released a sigh. "I wanted to catch him so badly."

"I don't even want to talk about you trying to catch the killer anymore," Jacque said.

"We won't talk about it right now," she agreed. "To be honest, right now, I couldn't fight my way out of a wet paper bag."

"Good to know. So if you misbehave, I could put a wet paper bag over your head and stop you in your tracks."

Her eyebrows raised slightly. "Oh my gosh, Jacque, did you just make a joke?" She released a small laugh and then groaned and grabbed her ribs. "I was beginning to wonder if you had a sense of humor."

"I only pull it out for special occasions," he replied with an unfamiliar grin.

"A joke and a smile. Wow, it's a stellar day."

He considered himself a loner, but he had to admit he was enjoying the conversation with her. "It's going to be time for lunch soon. Are ham sandwiches okay?"

"That's fine. I'll pay you for the extra groceries you're using to feed me."

"I've got it, Monique. I don't need your money."

"I pay my own way, Jacque."

"We'll argue about it on another day," he replied. "Don't make me get out the wet paper bag."

She laughed once again. "Okay, no more arguing."

There was no way he intended to take any money from her. He had plenty of his own, and he knew how hard she worked at her job.

The day passed pleasantly. They ate lunch and continued to talk. She shared with him her experiences growing up in the swamp and told funny stories about her and her sisters. In turn, he told her some stories of his childhood as an only child with a doting father and mother.

Daniel showed up just after lunch and asked Monique again about the attack, but she had nothing new to add. She couldn't give any kind of an identification and had no other information. He told them that he and his men had searched all around her porch and the surrounding area, but they had found nothing that could be used as evidence.

"What can you tell me about the note that was in the

box on your porch? I asked Jacque about it last night, but he said I'd need to talk to you," Daniel said.

She looked down at her lap and then back at the lawman. "I can't tell you anything about it," she replied. "I have no idea what it means or who could have left it." Her cheeks flushed lightly with the lie.

Minutes later Daniel left after promising to stay in touch. The fact that she hadn't come clean to Daniel concerned Jacque. What was the point in keeping it all a secret now? Unless at some point she thought she might go back to investigating again. Over my dead body, he thought.

At three Jacque gave her another pain pill, and after that she napped off and on. It was just after six when he went into the kitchen to fix dinner. He decided to fry up some fish and make some cheesy rice and corn to go with it.

She was napping, and as he thought of the day, he was pleased it had gone as smoothly as it had. He had a feeling she was going to be a very easy houseguest.

The only difficulty he might have was fighting against the simmering sexual tension she evoked in him. There was something about her that made him think of hot kisses and tangled bed sheets during lovemaking. But he told himself he was a strong man and the last thing he wanted was a relationship of any kind. His sole job right now was to keep her safe from a killer and that was it.

She awoke again as he was ready to plate the food. She went into the bathroom and then came to sit at the table. "It looks great," she said as he placed her plate before her.

"It's nothing special," he replied.

"It's special because you cooked it," she replied with one of her generous smiles that warmed him up inside.

"Oh, you're really on your best behavior," he replied dryly.

"Don't make me laugh." Her eyes sparkled merrily. "And of course I'm on my best behavior. I don't want you to kick me out of here just yet."

"Yet? Are you expecting a time will come when I will kick you out?" he asked.

"Maybe, but hopefully I won't be here long enough for that time to come. I intend to be out of here before I wear out my welcome." She took a bite of her fish. "Realistically, I can't impose on you until Daniel and his men make an arrest."

"Right now, we'll just take things day by day," he replied. He didn't want to argue with her about how long he intended her to stay with him. He wanted…he absolutely needed to keep her safe. Any other option was completely abhorrent and wasn't to be considered. He didn't care how long she had to stay here.

They fell into a comfortable silence as they ate. He welcomed the quiet. He had talked more today than he had in the past few months.

Once they were finished with the meal, he sent her back to the sofa and then he cleaned up the kitchen. He then went outside to shut off his generator and lit the lanterns. After, he returned to his chair across from her.

"It feels like I slept half the day away. I'm surprised I feel a little sleepy now," she said.

"That's your body trying to heal itself," he replied.

"When I'm sleeping, it's the only time I'm not in pain."

"Monique, I'm so damned sorry this happened to you," he said intently.

"It wasn't your fault," she replied. "I was the stupid person who stepped out on my porch in the dark." She released a small sigh. "Even though I got that note of warning, for some reason I just never dreamed the killer would actually come after me."

Lord knows, he'd tried to warn her that they were in too deep. "I'd still like to know how he caught on to what we were doing." He frowned.

"I swear I didn't tell anyone," she replied quickly.

"I believe you. And neither did I."

"Then it's a mystery how he figured it out."

"I don't like mysteries," he replied darkly.

"Trust me, neither do I."

They fell silent once again. He could tell she was hurting badly. She leaned back against the sofa cushion, and her eyes were dull and without their usual shine. Her arms were wrapped around her middle.

"Why don't you take a pill and go on to bed?" he suggested, hating to see her in such pain.

She frowned. "I hate taking the pain pills. I don't want to get addicted."

"Monique, you aren't going to get addicted, and right now you need them." He got out of his chair. "I'll go get you a glass of water so you can take one." A moment later he handed her the water and watched as she took one of the pills. "Now, go to bed, and I'll see you in the morning."

Slowly, she stood. "Thank you, Jacque, for taking such good care of me today. I really appreciate everything you're doing." With that, she disappeared into his guest bedroom and closed the door behind her.

He sat and relaxed back in his chair. Without her in the room, some of the tension that had been inside him all day slowly began to release. He wasn't accustomed to sharing his space with another person. He'd forgotten how pleasant it could be to have real conversations. She was very easy to talk to, and that made it easier on him.

With the day nearly over, he took his shoulder holster off and set it on the table next to him. Most nights at this time, he would grab his pole and do a little fishing.

Even though the water where he fished was relatively close to the back door of his shanty, he didn't think it was a good idea for him to go out and leave her in here alone, especially since apparently a killer wanted her dead.

He got up and turned off a few of the lanterns in the room, leaving only two on next to him. Then once again, he picked up the book he'd been reading. He didn't know how long he'd been lost in the story when he heard it…a loud rustling around his back door.

A rush of adrenaline suddenly exploded in his veins as he put his book down and instead picked up his gun. The rustling sounded like either a big animal or a human.

It wasn't uncommon to run into a sounder of wild boar in the swamp. The bulky, massively built pigs rooted on the ground and destroyed much of the vegetation. However, it was definitely unusual for them to come so close to a shanty.

That was also the case with the coyotes and bobcats in the area. Generally, they preferred to avoid humans at all costs. Still, something or someone was out there.

He rose from the chair, his gun gripped tightly in his

hand. He walked to the back door and quietly unlocked it. He threw it open and then took a step outside.

The shadowy figure of a man was there. A killer come to call? "Who's out here?" Jacque barked.

"Don't shoot… Jacque, it's me." George Trahan stepped into the faint light that came from Jacque's kitchen.

"Dammit, George, what the hell are you doing skulking around my back door?" Jacque slowly lowered his gun to point at the ground.

"I heard Monique was staying here with you and that she'd been beaten up pretty bad. I just wanted to see how she's doing."

"So, why not knock on my front door like a normal person?" Jacque asked with obvious irritation.

"I didn't want to bother her if she was really hurt, so I thought I'd just peek in the windows to see if she looked like she might be up for some company."

"That's a good way to get yourself shot," Jacque replied.

"I'm sorry, man. It was a bad decision on my part," George replied. "So, is she up for some company?"

"Actually, she's already gone to bed. If you want to see her, then I suggest you try tomorrow earlier in the day. And the next time you show up here, come to the front door," Jacque added.

"Will do," George replied. "I'll see you tomorrow, Jacque, and again, I'm really very sorry."

A few moments later Jacque sank back down in his chair, his thoughts racing. Was it possible George was the man they sought? He was swamp, not town, but Jacque could be wrong in guessing the killer was somebody prominent in town.

He knew George had initially been a suspect in Mystique's murder case. George had dated Angelique, and Mystique hadn't thought the gator-hunter was good enough for her daughter, voicing her thoughts directly to George.

Even though Angelique had stopped seeing George long before her mother's murder, was it possible George had held a grudge…a murderous grudge that resulted in slitting Mystique's throat? Had he believed Mystique was the reason Angelique had broken up with him?

Was it really possible that beneath his benign, easygoing ways, George was the monster? Had he killed Mystique and beaten Monique? And was the monster now looking for a way in to get at Monique once again?

Chapter Seven

Monique awakened to the sound of a soft rain pattering against the window. She slowly sat up, grateful that her pain was a little less intense than it had been the day before. Her ribs still hurt terribly, but the pain felt more manageable at the moment.

She gazed out the nearby window where the skies were gray with heavy clouds. She wondered if it was supposed to rain all day, not that it mattered to her. She certainly had no place to go.

However, she would like to get a shower today. As long as it wasn't lightning, she could shower in the rain. But how awkward was that going to be? Her cheeks flushed with warmth as she thought of being naked with Jacque so nearby.

Of course, she knew he'd be respectful, and her shower would go off without a hitch. Besides, despite her intense physical attraction to Jacque, she wasn't interested in any kind of relationship with him except his friendship, and of course, his protection for now.

She put on the same clothes as the day before, hoping to get out of them after her shower. As with the day before, she sneaked into the bathroom to wash her teeth and brush her hair. Minutes later she left the bedroom and stepped into the living area where she saw him seated at the table with a cup of coffee in front of him.

For a moment he didn't seem to hear her approach. His focus was directed out the nearby window. She took the moment to study him. He was such a handsome man and seemed to be so unaware of his own attractiveness.

Why had he chosen this solitary life for himself? Why wasn't an intelligent, handsome man like him married? What in his life had stolen his smiles? His laughter and joy?

She must have made a noise for his head suddenly swiveled around to look at her. "Good morning," she said.

"Good morning," he replied. "You sneaked up on me." He started to get up from the table, but she waved him back down.

"I can get my own coffee. All you need to do is point me to the cabinet with the cups."

"On the right side of the sink."

She opened the cabinet and pulled down one of the coffee mugs. She poured herself a cup and added a teaspoon of sugar from the sugar bowl on the counter. She then carried her cup to the table and sat across from him.

"I didn't know it was supposed to rain this morning," she said as she wrapped her fingers around the warmth of her mug.

"According to the weather report, it's going to be like this all day long," he replied.

"I hate gray, rainy days," she said. "It's like the whole world is frowning."

"Just think about how good the rain is for the trees and plants," he countered.

"Oh, I know rain is good, I just wish it would rain

only at night and then the sun would be bright by morning," she replied.

He cast her a half grin. "When you're in charge of the world, you can make that happen."

"Ha, if I was in charge of the world, there would be a lot more important things for me to take care of than when it rained," she replied.

"You're obviously feeling a bit better this morning. You look a little better except for that colorful bruise on your chin," he said.

She reached up and touched the sore spot. "I just wish I could have delivered a one-two punch back, but I never got the chance. As far as how I'm feeling, yesterday I felt like I'd been run over by a semitruck. Today I feel like I've been run over by a small car."

"That's progress," he replied. "Maybe by tomorrow you'll just feel like you were run over by a skateboard."

"One can only hope," she replied.

"I was thinking of making some pancakes for breakfast. How does that sound?"

"Sounds delicious. Just tell me what I can do to help."

"You can sit here and stay out of my way." He got up and stepped over to the kitchen cabinet that held his cookstove.

He pulled it out, then grabbed a box of pancake mix from the pantry closet. While the skillet was warming up, he placed butter and a big bottle of syrup on the table. It didn't take long before he had a large stack of pancakes ready to serve.

The rain continued to patter against the windows as they ate. They small-talked between bites, discussing favorite breakfast dishes. His favorite was bacon and eggs, and she was partial to cheese omelets. However, they both admitted a fondness for anything that required syrup.

She wanted to talk to him about the people who were still on their list of potential suspects and the few names she had added, but she decided to wait until later in the afternoon. She had a feeling the conversation might irritate him.

"Don't forget that tomorrow I'm going to work my shift at the store," she said as he was cleaning up the breakfast dishes.

He turned around to look at her, his green eyes radiating his disapproval. "Are you sure you're going to be up to it?"

"I need to be there. I need to place a couple of orders," she said. "It's important I be there as the manager of the store."

"The manager?" He looked at her in surprise. "When did that happen?"

She realized she hadn't told him about her promotion. "It happened on the day that I found the note on my front door."

"Congratulations," he replied. "I know how much you wanted it, and I know how hard you worked to earn it."

"Thank you, I've very happy about it, but that's why it's important for me to be there. Besides, I want to show everyone that I'm still alive and standing. That's important to me. I don't want anyone to think of me as weak. At least it's a relatively short shift."

"How short?" He finished with the dishes and gestured her into the living area.

"My shift is from nine in the morning until two." She

sat down on the sofa. At least for now she didn't feel like she needed a pain pill. She hurt, but at the moment her pain wasn't overwhelming.

"Personally, I don't think you're physically ready for that, but I know not to try to argue with you because you're a stubborn little…uh…woman." He sat in his recliner.

She laughed and then winced as pain shot through her ribs. "You're right, it wouldn't do you any good to argue with me. However, I do have a big favor to ask you. I'd really like to take a quick shower."

"No problem. It's a good time since the rain will help, that is if it's warm enough." He explained to her how to turn the water on in the shower. "When do you want to do this?"

"Now, if that's okay with you."

"It's fine by me. I'll just go get you a bath towel. The soap and shampoo bottles are in the stall."

"And I'll go change into a robe."

Thank goodness she had thrown a sleeveless, terry-cloth short robe in her bag before coming here. She changed into the robe and then met him by the back door where he waited with a huge black fluffy towel.

"The rain has stopped for now." He handed her the towel. "There are a couple of hooks right outside the stall. You can hang your things up there."

"Thanks, Jacque." She stepped out of the door and onto the deck. The air smelled good and fresh as if the rain had washed everything clean. The plants and bushes around the deck looked sparkling green, and it all made her eager to get a shower to make her as clean as the outside world.

The shower was much like the one she had at her shanty. She hung her towel and then stepped into the square structure and removed her robe. She reached out and hung it up next to where she had hung her towel. There was a shelf inside that held a bottle of fresh-scented soft soap and a bottle of shampoo.

The shower felt wonderful despite the water being a bit cool. She washed quickly, still surprised by how many bruises her body sported. They were up and down her legs and all over her ribs. If she dwelled on their presence for too long, she would be a total basket case.

She washed and rinsed her hair, then dried off and put her robe back on. By that time, it had begun to spit rain again, so she grabbed the towel and hurried inside.

"Here, I'll take that." Jacque got out of his chair and took the damp towel from her.

"Thanks, I'll be right back." She hurried on into her bedroom. She dressed in a pair of lightweight turquoise jogging pants and a turquoise and white T-shirt. It took a few minutes for her to brush out her wet hair and then she returned to the sofa.

"Better?" he asked.

"So much better," she replied. She offered him a bright smile, but he didn't return it. Instead, he frowned.

"I couldn't help but notice the bruising on your legs," he said, his scowl drawing his dark eyebrows closer together. "I can't even imagine how badly bruised your ribs are."

"They are a little black and blue. The bruises on my legs don't hurt that much," she replied. "And before you know it, they'll be gone."

His scowl eased somewhat. "Are you always so optimistic?"

"I try to be. Mom always told us that we could choose to be either happy or sad. So, most days I choose to be happy. You might try it sometime."

"How friendly are you with George Trahan?"

She looked at him, surprised by the unexpected question and unsurprised by him ignoring her final statement. "I'm always friendly when we run into each other, but I wouldn't consider him a close friend of mine. Why?"

"Last night after you went to bed, he came skulking around my back door. He said he was peeking in to see if it was a good time for him to come in and visit with you and make sure you were okay."

"That's a bit odd, but George has been a little off ever since his girlfriend tried to kill my sister. Maybe my attack brought back some bad memories, and he wanted to check on me."

"Maybe," he replied dubiously. "Or is it possible George killed your mother and he found out what we were doing by eavesdropping at my shanty's open windows?"

George? Was it possible he had not only murdered her mother but he'd also tried to beat her to death? A small shiver worked up her spine at this thought.

"At this point I think anything is possible," she finally replied. "The one thing that does make sense is how somebody knew what we were up to in getting the donated books. Somebody must have heard our conversation through your open windows."

"That's the one thing that finally makes sense," he agreed.

"I'd like to pick your brain about the rest of the people we had on our list of suspects. I've also got a couple of names to add."

"How about we eat lunch first and then we can talk about it?" he replied. "That way if the conversation makes me lose my appetite, I will have already eaten." He got out of his chair, and she followed him into the kitchen area.

"What can I do to help?" she asked.

"Nothing. It's just going to be sandwiches again," he said.

"That's fine with me."

They ate their sandwiches and then returned to the living room. Her pain came on a little stronger, and she would have liked to take a pill. But she wanted to talk to Jacque and feared she'd fall asleep in the middle of the conversation if she took one. They definitely made her sleepy.

"Okay, let's get into this," he said with a bit of reluctance in his tone.

"The evening that I was attacked, Jackson Scott came into the store to buy something for his latest honey. Do you know him?"

"I've seen him around, but I don't know him personally," Jacque said. "There are very few people I know in town."

"As far as I'm concerned, he's not only the district attorney but he's also a major sleazebag. He picks out a woman and love-bombs her for a couple of dates and then breaks up with her and moves on to his next victim."

"Sounds like a real piece of work," Jacque replied dryly.

"Yeah, anyway, for the first time ever, he asked what I was up to when I wasn't working at the store. It was odd for him to ask me that."

"Why would he want to kill your mother?"

"This is only a wild supposition on my part, but what I was thinking was maybe he was a client of my mother's and somehow he got scared that she was going to tell his secrets. And I even speculated on what his secret might be."

"What's that?"

"Erectile dysfunction."

He stared at her for a long moment and then threw back his head and began to laugh. It was a full-blown deep laugh she'd never heard from him before. It rumbled pleasantly in the air, and she loved the sound of it and the way his green eyes lit up with his mirth.

"I'm sorry," he finally said as he sobered. "Of all the things I expected you to say, that wasn't one of them."

"But think about it," she continued. "He has a real playboy reputation. Maybe he dates the women until it's time for him to have sex with them, but because he can't perform, he just breaks up with them."

"I suppose that could be right," he replied. "So who else have you been thinking about?"

"Charles Lathrop was initially on the cop's suspect list and as far as I've heard he's still on it. He's a wealthy businessman who came to my mother for a love spell."

"Yeah, I remember. The spell didn't work, and he was angry with your mother. What do you think about him?"

She frowned thoughtfully. "I'm not quite sure what to think about him. I've heard that he's an arrogant ass, but my gut says he isn't the killer. Still, he should continue to be on our suspect list. The only other person left on our original suspect list is Jeb Tyler, the owner of the bank."

"Was he seeing your mother?" Jacque asked.

"I have no idea, but he is a prominent member of town who might have secrets he didn't want exposed. That ends the list we had made, but I've thought of a few others to add." She winced as she shifted positions, her pain ever-present.

"And who would those be?"

"First of all is Greg Hatterly, who is on the city council. Secondly is Hugh Lauren, who owns the Voodoo Lounge and last is Howard Griffen, who owns the grocery store."

"Speaking of the grocery store, when I pick you up after work tomorrow, we need to stop in there so I can get some groceries."

"What do you mean when you pick me up after work?"

Once again, his gaze was intent as it held hers. "I will be taking you to work and picking you up afterward," he replied.

"Oh, Jacque, surely I can drive myself without any issues," she protested.

"Nope, not going to happen," he said firmly.

"You didn't sign up for all this."

"Yes, I did," he replied with a little bit of terseness in his tone. "When I signed on to help you with your plan, I also signed on to deal with whatever came up. Somebody tried to kill you, and I'm not going to allow that to happen."

"I wonder why they aren't going after you?" she mused.

"Probably because you're the brains of the operation

and whoever is after you knows that if you're no longer around, our little investigation will stop."

"You wouldn't keep investigating to see who killed me?" She shifted positions once again.

He released a deep sigh. "I've already done at least a thousand investigations in my lifetime. I would probably tell Daniel everything I know and then leave it up to him. That's what we need to do now."

She ignored his last statement and instead focused on the first thing he had said. "At least a thousand investigations? What does that mean?"

He broke eye contact with her and instead gazed at some point over her shoulder. "In my former life before coming to the swamp, I was a Baton Rouge homicide detective."

He hadn't really wanted to share that information with anyone here in Dark Waters. He was aware of her staring at him in stunned surprise. He finally returned his gaze to hers.

"I knew it," she said softly, her eyes still widened in response to his confession. "I knew you were smarter than the average Joe when it comes to these matters. What made you quit that job to move to the swamp?"

He felt as if he'd opened up a whole can of worms, and more than anything he wanted to put the lid back on. "Burnout," he replied curtly, hoping not to invite any more questions. "And I've watched you for the past twenty minutes squirming with pain. You need to take another pill."

She narrowed her beautiful eyes. "Are you wanting

me to take a pill in the hopes that I'll fall asleep and stop talking…stop asking questions?"

"Maybe," he replied. "But I can also see that you're in a lot of pain."

"I am," she admitted. She leaned forward and grabbed the pill bottle from the coffee table.

"I'll go get you a glass of water." He got up from the chair and a moment later handed her the glass.

She shook out a pill and chased it down with the water, then handed him back the glass. "I still have questions for you. Jacque, I'd like to know you better. I believe you're worth knowing better," she said, her voice soft and her gaze caring.

It touched him. She touched him, and he hated it. "Get some rest," he replied gruffly.

She read on her phone for about twenty minutes and then fell asleep. He used the quiet time in an effort to recenter himself.

The fact that he had a strong physical attraction to her coupled with the fact that he genuinely liked her was a dangerous combination. He didn't want to like her, and he definitely wished his intense desire for her would just go away. The last thing he wanted was to really care for her. The last time he'd cared about someone really bad things had happened.

Afraid of where his mind was taking him, he got up and went to the kitchen table.

He stared outside the window. Rain still came down from the heavy gray clouds. At the moment, they reflected his mood. The talk about the people left on their suspect list had concerned him.

He hoped like hell she didn't intend to continue visiting those homes for an opportunity to search for her mother's book. After being beaten up so badly, surely she would recognize the amount of danger she would be in if she continued on that path. She was stubborn, but she certainly wasn't stupid.

And who had beat her? God, he would love to know. It took a special kind of man to beat up a woman. Who had killed the voodoo queen, Mystique? That murder was what had set into play these dire circumstances for Monique.

It had been just about four months now since the murder. Jacque knew from his own experience as a cop that once a case went on that long it grew cold. Leads dried up, and people's memories faded. There was a possibility now that the crime might never be solved.

As far as who had beaten Monique? There were no clues to follow, Daniel had told him they had tried to identify where the box that had been left on her porch had come from but so far they had been unsuccessful. The note inside had been handwritten and hadn't been matched to a particular person. So it was equally possible her case might not be solved as well. Jacque had never liked loose ends, and this was one he definitely didn't like. Dammit, these crimes needed to be solved by law enforcement and not by a beautiful woman all on her own.

Now that he realized the assailant could have learned about what they were doing by listening at his windows, the possibility that a person from the swamp was the killer was a very real thing.

He shoved all these thoughts away. He hadn't had a

moment of complete peace since the minute he agreed to help Monique. She had brought chaos into his life.

She had also brought a warmth and vibrant energy that he'd been missing for a very long time. She made him smile and reclaim his sense of humor.

He released a deep sigh. All he really knew was he was tired of thinking about murder and mayhem. And he definitely didn't want to think about his desire for the woman sleeping on his sofa.

She slept for about an hour and awakened with her beautiful smile in place. "I feel so much better," she said as she swung her legs around to sit up.

When she'd come in from her shower, he'd not only noticed the bruising on her skin but also that her legs were slender and shapely.

"I'm glad you feel better," he replied. "I think I'm going to go ahead and get started on dinner. How does spaghetti with sauce and shrimp sound?"

"Delicious," she replied. "I wish you'd let me help you. I feel guilty just sitting at the table and letting you do all the work."

"Don't feel guilty. I cook every evening for myself, and it's no trouble to make the meal for two. Besides, the kitchen is too small to have the both of us in it."

He didn't want her that close to him where he could feel her body heat radiating toward him and where they might inadvertently touch each other. He didn't want to be so close to her delicious scent as it threatened to dizzy his senses. He didn't want her anywhere near him as he was feeling particularly vulnerable right now. He'd spent far too much time this afternoon thinking about what her lips would taste like and how her naked skin would feel against his own.

She was bruised all over, had two fractured ribs, and he was thinking about sex. He was ashamed of his own thoughts. He got up from the table and moved into the kitchen area where he couldn't see her.

"I'll sit in here and keep you company," she said as she sat at the table.

So much for his brief escape from her presence. He stepped outside the back door and started his generator, then got out his cooktop and plugged it in. From his pantry, he pulled out a pound of spaghetti and a jar full of sauce.

"Before you forced me to go to sleep, you told me you quit being a homicide detective because of burnout. Was it one particular case that really got to you?" she asked.

He wished he'd never opened this door, but he had, and of course she had questions for him. It had certainly been one event that had made him walk away from his job, but it had nothing to do with his work. But he wasn't about to go down that path.

"No, it wasn't any one particular case. I guess it was just an accumulation of all of them." He filled a pot with water and put in on the burner to boil, then emptied the jar of sauce into a pan and placed it on the stove to warm. "It's a job where you definitely see the horror that human beings can do to each other."

"How long were you on the force?" she asked.

"Almost eight years." He pulled the bag of cooked shrimp out of the cooler and set it next to the saucepan. "I was hired on when I had just turned twenty-one."

"Then that makes you thirty-three years old?" It was more a question than a comment.

"That's right," he agreed.

"Have you ever been married?"

"Yeah, once."

"What happened?" she asked, curiosity rife in her tone.

"It didn't work out." A wealth of deep emotion built up inside him. He swallowed hard against it and tried to push it away, but it tightened his chest and made it difficult for him to breathe.

"I'm sorry," she replied in that soft, gentle tone that always got to him.

"What about you? I'm pretty sure you've never married, but have you had a serious relationship before?" He would much prefer that the conversation be about her instead of himself.

"I've had one serious relationship, but it didn't work out. That was two years ago, and since then my main focus has been about my work. Until my mother's murder, I really had no other focus."

"Now that you're the store manager, what's next for you career-wise? Are you now where you want to be for the rest of your working life?" He turned to glance at her.

She looked so lovely in the turquoise and white T-shirt. It was a perfect color for her dark beauty. Even without makeup, he could see the dark length of her eyelashes and the natural blush in her cheeks. He turned back to the stovetop as his gut tightened for another reason altogether.

"Yes and no," she replied. "What I'm really hoping is that eventually Debbie will be ready to sell the shop and step away from it altogether. I've been saving and hope that when that day comes, I can buy the store from her."

"So, you want to be a shop owner."

"That would be my ultimate dream," she replied. "Once that happens, I'll be ready to devote more time to my social life."

As the water in the pot began to boil, Jacque broke the noodles in half and put them in the water. He opened the bag of shrimp, rinsed them off and put them in the sauce.

"Of course, I'm hoping by that time my mother's case will be solved," she added.

"And hopefully you're planning on forgetting about your own investigating skills." He stirred the spaghetti and then turned to face her once again.

"I haven't decided that yet."

He looked at her in surprise. "Please tell me you aren't going to try to continue what you've been doing."

"Probably not, but I need to do something to find the killer."

He looked at her in frustration. "Monique, you need to stay as far as you can away from anything to do with this. You got lucky that a neighbor heard you scream when you were getting beaten. You might not be as lucky next time."

"I know, but I hate to feel like I failed." She looked down at the table. "It's like my sisters have always thought about me. I'm the baby of the family and too weak and incompetent to do anything but sell pretty clothes. If I could solve my mother's murder, then maybe they would change the way they view me."

Her words surprised him as they revealed what was obviously a driving reason for her desire to solve Mystique's murder. He would have never guessed that she was somehow trying to prove herself to her older siblings.

"Monique, you didn't fail. I don't know for sure how somebody found out what we were doing, but you were warned to stop it. Still, you pushed on and then you got beat up. Good God, woman, you've shown yourself to be incredibly strong and courageous. That's definitely not a fail. However now you would really be a fool to continue on and deep down you've got to know that."

"You're boiling over."

He looked at her in confusion. "What?"

"Your pot… It's boiling over."

He quickly turned around to lower the burner and then began to stir the cooking noodles in an effort to make it stop boiling out of the pot. Once he had that under control, he stirred the sauce, then set a bag of bread and a tub of butter on the table.

"Do you want me to make a salad?" he asked.

"No, I'd rather eat extra spaghetti and not spoil it by eating a salad."

"Then you're my kind of woman," he replied lightly.

It didn't take long for the meal to be ready to serve. As they ate, she asked him about the investigations he'd done, and he found himself telling her about some of the more humorous things he and his partner had gone through.

He liked to make her laugh. For the past four years there had been no real laughter here. She had such a musical one and it seemed to fill up all the dark corners in his shanty.

He was almost grateful when the meal was over. He cleaned up the dishes, went to sit in his chair and immediately picked up his book. He was done talking to her for the night. He'd already opened himself up far too much.

He was aware of her gaze on him as he opened the book. She must have gotten the message for she picked up her phone and began reading something on it.

He found his thoughts wandering as he stared at the words on the page. Tomorrow they would begin a new routine with her insisting on going back to work. He still thought it was too early for her to return, but he also knew there was no way he could talk her out of going. He could definitely protect her to and from work.

Would somebody come after her while she was in the store? His gut instinct told him no. The store was on Main Street and according to Monique it kept fairly busy. He didn't think the killer would want to chance going into a public place to get to her.

Was it possible the killer would leave Monique alone now? He'd like to think so, but he couldn't be sure. And his uncertainty would keep her here and safe. But he had to somehow keep his distance from her. She was far too easy to talk to, far too charming and beautiful, and it threatened the solitary life he'd built for himself.

So the real question was while he was keeping her safe, who was going to keep him safe from her?

Chapter Eight

At eight forty-five the next morning, she and Jacque got into his car and headed toward town. "Hopefully, you'll have a peaceful day at work," he said.

"Hopefully." She gazed at him for a long moment. He looked as handsome as ever in jeans and a short-sleeved mint green polo that really brought out the bright green of his eyes. "And hopefully you'll have some peaceful hours while I'm gone," she replied.

She turned her gaze out the window, her thoughts going to the day before. She had enjoyed the funny stories he'd shared about his work over dinner. It was a tantalizing glimpse into his former life and the man he had been before coming to the swamp.

However, immediately after dinner he'd closed himself off, and it had been quite obvious he'd wanted no more conversation. She couldn't be upset about it. She was a guest in his home. If he didn't feel like talking, then so be it.

But she couldn't help but wonder what drove his mood to change. She still sensed pain deep inside his soul. Had he lied about why he'd left police work? Had there been a particularly bad case that hurt him so deeply that for his own sanity he'd needed to step away? Or was it something else altogether?

She wished he would share more with her. Despite his moodiness, she genuinely cared about him. In fact, she cared about him maybe more than she should.

He fascinated and intrigued her. She wanted to know everything there was to learn about him. There was no reason why, when this was all over, they couldn't remain close friends. She could definitely use one, but she couldn't be sure he would want that. He was so darned hard to read.

She shifted positions and stifled a groan of discomfort. There was no question she was still in pain, but it wasn't quite as bad as it had been. Slowly she was healing. The bruising on her legs and chin had changed from purple to yellow, indicating that they were getting better. Even her ribs felt a little better. Although they still hurt a lot, it wasn't the horrible stabbing and burning she had felt over the last couple of days.

Her sisters had continued to call to check up on her. There was no question they were worried about her, but she had discouraged them from coming to visit. Besides, there was nothing they could do for her.

"By the way, you look nice today," he surprised her by saying as they pulled up in front of the store.

Thankfully she had put the long navy skirt and a red and navy blouse in her bag when she'd packed. "Thanks," she replied. "If you don't mind, maybe after work today we could stop by my shanty so I could grab a few more clothes for workdays."

"I don't see a problem with that," he replied.

"What do you have planned while I'm in the store slaving away?" she asked.

"I thought I'd stop into the police station and see if I can have a chat with Daniel about your attack and then I'm going to go ahead and get some groceries," he replied.

"Are you going to tell him you used to be a homicide detective?"

"I'm not sure. I haven't decided yet," he replied.

"When we stop by my shanty later, I'll get you some money for the groceries," she replied. She certainly didn't intend to be a freeloader while staying with him. He pulled to a stop along the curb in front of the store.

"We can talk about all that later. Monique, if there's a moment in the shop where you don't feel safe or you don't feel well enough to work, call me and I'll come to you immediately."

"I will." She smiled at him. "Thanks for the ride, and I'll see you at two." With that, she opened the car door and got out.

He waited to pull away from the curb until she was safely inside and only then did he take off.

She went about the business of opening the store, turning on lights and then flipping the sign on the door from Closed to Open.

While she waited for the first customers, she retrieved the work computer from the back room and carried it back to the counter next to the register. There was a warehouse in New Orleans that sold a particular brand of clothing she'd been wanting to get into the shop. Now that she was officially the manager with buying power, she was going to pick out a few items to bring in and test the waters here.

She quickly got lost in the fashion on screen. She loved seeing new designs and outfits that were fresh and unique. It was only when the tinkle of the bell sounded over the front door that she looked up to see Nola coming in.

"Hi, darling," she greeted Monique. Her smile faded as she got closer and she noticed Monique's bruised chin. "Oh, my poor baby," she exclaimed. "I wanted to come by and check on you sooner, but to be honest I'm a little bit afraid of Jacque."

"Auntie Nola," Monique said, using the childhood name she'd always called her mother's friend. "I always thought you weren't afraid of anything," she teased.

"Honey, there's plenty of things that scare me, including that big man who lives deep in the swamp. He wears such a scowl on his face all the time. Now, tell me how you're doing? I'm surprised to see you here at work. I heard you took quite a beating."

"I did," Monique confessed. "I've got a couple of fractured ribs and a body full of bruises."

Nola frowned. "I'm so sorry, honey. And you have no idea who did this to you?"

"I don't have a clue."

"If you find out, then let me know." Nola raised her fists in a fighting position and punched out with her right hand. "I'll take care of the person for you."

Monique laughed. "I don't think that will be necessary. Right now, I've got the scowling man from deep in the swamp watching over me."

"Tell me, what on earth is going on in your life that

you're getting beat up and you need somebody to watch over you?" Nola gazed at her curiously.

For just a brief moment, Monique really wanted to tell Nola the truth about what she and Jacque had been up to, but in the end, she decided to keep it a secret even from the woman who had been like a mother to her.

"I haven't figured that out yet. Somehow, someway, I've made somebody very angry with me, but darned if I know who or why," Monique replied.

"Is Daniel looking into it?" Nola asked.

"Yes, he is. But there isn't much to look into. I couldn't give him a description of the attacker, and there was no evidence to be found around my front porch, where I was attacked." She didn't mention the box or note that was left on her porch.

Nola frowned. "I know your sister loves that man to distraction, but until he solves your mother's murder and now this mystery you're in, he is definitely on my bad side."

"Don't be too hard on him, Nola. We know he's working as hard as possible to get Mother's murderer in jail," Monique replied.

"I can't believe it's taken this long for him and his men to figure out who killed Mystique," Nola replied. "I'm worried now that it will never get solved."

"That makes two of us," Monique replied fervently.

"So, is Jacque treating you right?"

Monique smiled. "He's been very kind and considerate to me. He's really a very nice man."

"I'd believe you if he didn't look so fierce all the time," Nola replied.

At that moment, two teenage girls came into the shop.

"I think that's my cue to get on with my errands. Stay safe, Monique, and you know you can call or come talk to me anytime." She blew Monique a kiss and then turned and headed out the store door.

The teenagers were in the store for about half an hour, trying on different blouses and checking out the costume jewelry. One of them wound up buying a set of pink and gold bangle bracelets while the other one got a pretty bright yellow blouse.

It was just before lunch when her two sisters came through the door.

"I couldn't believe it when Nola came into my store a little while ago and told me you were at work today," Angelique said, worry evident on her features.

"And I couldn't believe it when Angelique called and told me," Dominique added, also looking deeply concerned.

"Shouldn't you be at Jacque's and resting more?" Angelique asked.

"I needed to get back to work," Monique replied. "Besides, it's not like this is tough physical labor."

"Are you in a lot of pain?" Dominique asked with sympathy.

"Yes, I am. But it's getting better with every day that passes," Monique replied.

"Still, you shouldn't be pushing yourself too hard," Angelique chided her.

"I'm a big girl, sis, and I can make decisions about myself," Monique replied with a tad bit of irritation.

"Oh, I know." Angelique smiled in an obvious apology. "I just worry about you."

Monique's irritation immediately faded away. "I'm

getting along just fine," she said. "Besides, in less than two hours I'll be back on Jacque's sofa and resting."

"So, you're comfortable there?" Dominique asked.

"Very comfortable, and he's committed to making sure I stay safe," Monique replied.

"I can tell you Daniel is absolutely tearing his hair out with frustration over Mama's case and now yours," Angelique said.

"And you have no idea why somebody attacked you?" Dominique asked.

"No clue." This little white lie was falling easier and easier from her lips. Would it really help Daniel in his investigation if he knew what she and Jacque had been doing? Maybe it was time to come clean with Daniel. There was no question that their activities had given somebody a motive for murder.

Her sisters remained in the shop for about a half hour, and then Angelique needed to get back to her store and it was time for Dominique to head to the café for her shift.

Lunchtime came and went, and the shop stayed fairly busy until almost two when Cynthia came in to work. A look out of the front window let Monique see Jacque's car pull up at the curb.

When there had been lulls of customers in the shop, her thoughts had gone to the man who, at least for now, had put his own life on hold for hers.

She didn't have a ton of experience when it came to lust. She'd only had one lover in her life. But there was no question she had some major lust building up for Jacque, and it was something that had no place in their relationship as budding friends. She just needed to figure out a way to squash the physical attraction.

"Good day?" he asked as she slid into the passenger seat of his car.

"It was a good day," she agreed. "Nola stopped by, and then my sisters came in, which was enjoyable, and I stayed pretty busy, which is always nice. What about you? Good day?"

"Okay day." He pulled away from the curb. "After I dropped you off, I went to the police station and spoke to Daniel. Unfortunately, there has been no movement in your mother's case or in yours."

"I figured that since he hadn't been by to talk to us," she replied.

"I'm just hoping he finds the perp before you get well enough to come up with another crazy plan."

She laughed. "Don't worry, right now another plan is the last thing on my mind."

He flashed her a quick glance. "That's good to know. After I spoke to Daniel, I went to the grocery store, and then I went home and put everything away, and now I'm here with you. And I haven't forgotten that you want to stop by your shanty on the way home."

"Yes, since I intend to continue going into work, I need to pick up some more of my clothes."

"How do you feel?" He shot her another quick glance and then returned his gaze to the road.

"I'm a bit tired, and I'm hurting some, but I'm all right," she replied.

"What's your schedule like for tomorrow?"

"The same as today." She studied his profile for a moment. "Jacque, how long are we going to do this?"

"Do what?" He shot her yet another quick glance.

"How long am I going to be staying at your shanty?

It isn't realistic for me to stay until Daniel catches the bad guy. That hasn't happened in the last four months, and it might never happen."

"Tired of my hospitality already?" One of his dark eyebrows quirked upward.

"Of course not," she quickly answered.

"Monique, please as I told you before, let's just take this one day at a time, okay? Right now, I really believe you are where you need to be."

Of course he was right. In truth, she was afraid to leave his protection. She had tried not to focus on her fear, but it was there simmering inside her all the time.

Was her mother's killer and the person who attacked her just lying in wait? Looking for a weakness in Jacque's protection that could be breached? Was that person now someplace nearby, plotting and planning on how to get to her again? And this time with deadly results? It was these kinds of thoughts that kept her afraid.

When they reached the swamp, he walked closely beside her until they reached her shanty. "Why don't you have a seat?" She gestured toward her sofa. "This will only take me a couple of minutes."

As he sat on the sofa, she went into her bedroom closet and began to pull out clothing that would be appropriate for work. In another bag, she placed a couple pairs of jeans and some more casual clothes. She always washed her clothes at the laundromat in town, and she assumed Jacque did, too. But he hadn't mentioned a trip there, so she wanted to have plenty of clean clothes with her. Once she had everything gathered together, she called out to Jacque.

He came into the bedroom.

"I was wondering if you could help me carry some of this," she asked.

"Of course." He stepped closer to her, so close that she could feel his warm breath on her face. Their gazes locked, and it was as if time suddenly stood still.

A crazy energy snapped in the air between them, and his eyes glowed with a fiery green light that sent her heartbeat racing. "Kiss me, Jacque." The words escaped her on a whisper.

His eyes flared, and he pulled her into his arms and took her mouth with his. White-hot fire raced through her veins as the kiss continued. She opened her mouth to him, and their tongues danced together in sweet unison. His lips were demanding and hungry, yet soft and definitely hot.

With a small groan, he dropped his arms and stepped back from her. His eyes still blazed with green flames before he broke eye contact. "That will never happen again," he said brusquely. "Now, tell me what all I need to carry."

A few minutes later he walked behind her with her stack of clothes in his arms. She held one of the bags and thought about the kiss they had just shared.

It had been incredibly hot and wonderful. But it had been far too short. She wished it had gone on much longer. It was hard to believe his pronouncement that he would never kiss her again, for she had seen the hunger in his eyes, and she had tasted his sizzling desire.

Despite her pain, what she really would have liked was if the kiss had been followed up by her pulling him to the bed where they would make mad, passionate love. Somehow, she knew that he would be an incredible lover.

She chided herself for these kind of thoughts. She told herself she just needed him for his friendship and protection. What she didn't understand was why she was so eager for more?

JACQUE WAS PISSED at himself and at her. He was angry at himself for losing control and kissing her, and he was angry with her for looking so damn kissable. He just hadn't been able to stop himself.

He'd known instinctively that her lips would be pillowy soft, yet incredibly hot. Now he knew for sure that was the case.

Kissing her had been intoxicating, but he'd sworn he would never kiss another woman, he'd vowed that he would never desire another woman. All he could do now was admit his mistake and make sure it never happened again.

When they reached his shanty, he followed her into her bedroom, placed the clothes on her bed, then he left. She stayed behind to put everything away.

He walked over to his back door, opened it and stepped out on his porch. He drew in a deep breath, needing to rid the sweet scent of her from his head. He needed to clear his mind from the very hot kiss they had just shared.

After a few minutes, he went into his bedroom and closed the door. He sank down on the edge of his bed, opened the nightstand drawer and pulled out the framed photo that was inside.

As he stared at it, the pain he'd worked so hard to get past rose up and squeezed him tight around his chest, making it difficult for him to breathe. He ran a finger over the glass that protected the photo, touching the images of people who were gone forever.

This was the reason he would never invite another woman into his life. This was the very reason he never wanted to kiss Monique again. He didn't want to care for her other than keeping her safe. He didn't deserve a woman's love.

He placed the photo back into the drawer, got up and went into the living room. Monique was still in her bedroom, which gave him some more time to breathe.

Closing his eyes and settling in his chair, he wrapped himself with old memories. He rarely allowed himself to go back in time. It hurt too much when he had to come back to the present.

However, for now he went back to a time when he was the happiest and had felt like he was on top of the world. There had been laughter and so much joy, and then there had been nothing but the aching grief that had consumed him.

Before he could get too swept away in the past, Monique came into the room. She had changed clothes and now wore a pair of jeans and a purple T-shirt advertising her sister's shop, Mystique's Magic. She sat down on the sofa and offered him a smile. "Mission accomplished. All my clothes have been put away and all is right with the kingdom."

He sat up straighter as he suddenly realized something. "I nearly forgot, but tonight is when the men usually come over for their lessons. I need to call George and see if he can let the men know it's canceled."

"Why cancel it? I can just stay in my bedroom while they're here."

"You wouldn't mind that?" he asked.

"Definitely not. Jacque, I don't want you to give up all of your life because of my presence here."

He stood. "Then I'm going to head in and make us an early dinner. The men usually start arriving at around five."

That night the men came and went without a hitch, and it was only after they left that Jacque realized George hadn't even asked about Monique. Odd that he would come around one night supposedly on the off chance of checking in on her and yet he had never followed through.

Over the next week, Jacque and Monique settled into a routine. He took her to and from work, he cooked dinner for them, and then the rest of the evening passed with small talk.

He was definitely trying to keep his distance from her. The thought of the kiss they had shared continued to plague him, playing and replaying in his mind over and over again.

Her floral scent permeated all the air in the shanty, and he was acutely aware of her every breath, her every sigh when they were together in a room.

There had been no word from Daniel about the murder or the attack on Monique. Jacque didn't know if Monique was still in danger or not, but he certainly wanted to err on the side of caution. Right now, he wasn't in any hurry to send her on her way despite the discomfort of his own sexual desire for her.

He could tell she was feeling better with each day that passed. She had stopped taking the pain pills and didn't wince as much when she moved.

"You know the fall festival is next week," she said. Once again, she was seated on the sofa and he was in his chair. She was wearing a pair of pink jogging pants and a pink T-shirt. Her hair was a dark curtain of silk down her back, and she looked achingly lovely.

"Yeah, when I was in town yesterday to get gasoline and ice for the cooler, that's all everyone was talking about," he replied.

"Have you ever been to one before?" she asked.

"No, I never really had any desire to go in the past." He hadn't wanted to put himself in a place where happy people gathered with their families. He hadn't wanted to hear their laughter when there was no laughter in his heart, in his life. "I'll bet you and your sisters all went before."

"We've gone every year since we were kids." Her eyes sparkled brightly. "It was always a real treat for us kids from the swamp. There was so much food to eat and cool things to look at, and of course there was the carnival."

"I suppose you all rode every ride," he said.

"Oh no. We didn't have enough money to do that. Mama would only give us a little bit of money. It was usually enough to get something to eat and ride on one ride. We always saved enough money to ride the Ferris wheel at night when it was all lit up with twinkling colorful lights."

"Sounds like you had fun," he replied.

"We did." She fell silent for just a moment, and he picked up his book. "Jacque?"

He looked back at her. "Yes?"

"I was wondering if maybe we could be in town for the fall festival. I'd like to run a sidewalk sale at the shop, and I wouldn't go anyplace else. So could we be there that day?"

He thought of all the logistics involved with such a plan. There would be tons of people on the streets, and he was relatively certain the murderer would be there. Would he make a move on Monique? Doubtful, especially if Jacque remained at her side wearing his gun.

Then there was his abhorrence to be at such a place with so many people, but as he saw the fragile hope in Monique's eyes. He couldn't deny her the pleasure. "Yeah, I think we could make that work."

"Thank you, Jacque," she replied. "I promise I won't even make you smile that day if you don't want to."

That made him laugh. She was getting to him. Her cheerfulness, her optimism and teasing were definitely causing a change in him.

There was no question that he smiled more, and her little quips often made him laugh. He wasn't sure he liked it. The more he enjoyed her company, the more difficult it would be when it came time to say goodbye.

And he would have to say goodbye. There would come a time when she would return to her shanty and her own life, and he would return to being the frowning loner of the swamp.

Chapter Nine

The day of the fair, the weather was absolutely perfect. The hot temperatures had cooled, making it comfortable to be outside. The sky was a perfect blue without a cloud in the sky. At eight in the morning, Monique and Jacque got into his car to head into town.

The past week with him had been confusing. One minute he was open and warm with her, and the next he was closed off and cold. She couldn't begin to guess what demons he had inside him. She wanted to discover what they were and somehow exorcize them. She wanted him warm and open with her all the time, but she didn't know how to make that happen.

Her ribs were definitely feeling better and the thought of returning to her shanty was happening more and more often. But today she didn't want to think of anything but having fun and enjoying the day.

"Are you ready for this?" she asked as she gazed at his handsome profile.

"As ready as I'll ever be," he replied with a quick smile at her.

As always, his smile blossomed a wave of warmth through her. Her desire for him continued to grow with each day that passed. She wanted him, and there were definitely times when she believed he wanted her, too.

There were moments when she felt him looking at her when he thought she didn't notice. There were also times when an inadvertent touch from him lingered for a bit too long. But she also didn't want to think about that today, either. These kinds of thoughts only confused her.

She directed him to park at the back of All That Jazz as parking on Main Street was discouraged on this special day of celebration. He turned off the engine, unfastened his seat belt and then turned to look at her.

"Let's go over the rules for the day," he said. "First of all, you stay close to me. Second, you don't leave the area with anyone but me."

"And third, I changed my mind. I need you to smile a bit today, otherwise you'll chase off all my customers with your scowls," she said.

He laughed. "Okay, I'll work on that."

"You don't have to worry about me wandering off from you," she added. "I'm well aware that I could still be in some kind of danger. But I don't want to even think about that today. It's a day for fun. Do you know how to have fun, Jacque?" she asked teasingly.

He gave her a half grin. "Just for you, I'll dig deep and see if I can remember how to have fun. Now we'd better get inside so you can get set up for this sidewalk sale you intend to have starting at nine."

Together they went into the store through the back door, and he immediately re-locked the door behind them. As she began pulling items off the racks and placing them on a separate rack that would go outside, he wandered around the shop.

"I don't go into women's stores, but this one looks really nice," he said.

"Thanks," she said with a huge sense of pride.

"What can I do to help you?" he asked.

"There's a card table in the back room. If you want to bring it up here, that would be great."

"Consider it done." He went down the short hallway and disappeared into the back room. It was not only where people could take their breaks, but it was also a storage room holding stock.

He returned with the card table.

"Just lean it against the door. I want to take it outside and use it along with this rack of clothing. But first I need to mark down the prices of the things that will be on sale. If you want, just have a seat behind the register."

He sat and watched as she worked with her calculator and changed the prices. "How much are you cutting the prices?"

"I'm marking them down by forty percent."

"That's a really good discount," he replied.

"Most of these items have been really slow sellers, so now the goal is just to get rid of them and make what I can," she replied. "Of course I got Debbie's permission to do all this."

"Just think, once you buy the shop you won't have to ask permission from anyone for anything," he said.

"We'll have to wait to see if that really happens, but that's certainly my goal," she replied wistfully. "I would love to own this shop."

It took her several minutes to get the clothes tagged with the sale price, and then she moved on to the scarves, jewelry and shoes she intended to sell. Once everything was tagged appropriately, she went into the back room and grabbed a black tablecloth to cover the card table. Finally, she was ready to move everything outside. It was an easy job with Jacque there to help her.

At all the other stores down Main Street, there was a flurry of activity as clerks and owners worked to set up for the sidewalk sale. In the distance a Ferris wheel rose up, and even though it was early in the day, the scents of popcorn, grilling hot dogs and other culinary delights filled the air.

It all had a thrumming energy that filled her with excitement. The sidewalk sale would last until five o'clock, and then all the stores would close, giving everyone time to enjoy the festivities.

She was working the entire day, although she had arranged for Samantha McGuire, a middle-aged woman she had recently hired, to work with her. She was hoping her sale would be so busy it would need two sales clerks.

At exactly nine o'clock Samantha showed up. She was an attractive woman and a frequent buyer at the store. Monique introduced Samantha to Jacque, and then Jacque brought three folding chairs from the back room and placed them beside the rack and card table.

The two women sat, but Jacque remained standing just behind Monique. Today he was wearing a pair of black slacks and a green-and black short-sleeved dress shirt. He also wore his shoulder holster and gun. He looked incredibly hot and a little bit dangerous. She found it a very sexy combination.

It wasn't long before the street began to fill with people. Laughter filled the air, along with the sounds of dozens of conversations.

Women started coming by their sale, thumbing through the clothes and checking out the other items. Some bought things while others were just lookers. The morning passed quickly with a lot of traffic and sales, and before Monique knew, it was after noon.

Jacque had remained a standing sentry just behind her all morning. She was pleased that he had actually smiled when customers approached, but she knew he was probably getting hungry.

There was a lull in the traffic, and she turned to Samantha. "You think you can handle things here by yourself for a few minutes while Jacque and I grab something for lunch? And then when we get back you can go to get some lunch."

"That sounds good to me," Samantha agreed. "I'll be fine here alone."

Monique stood from the chair and looked at Jacque. "You ready to see what we can find to eat?"

"Definitely," he replied.

"Then let's go."

There was still a crowd of people on the streets although a lot of folks were gathered in front of City Hall. A bandstand was set up there, and a local band was playing country tunes.

As they walked, Jacque surprised her by wrapping one of his arms around her shoulders and pulling her closer to his side. She knew he was doing so to make sure she stayed safe, but she found it more than wonderful to have his body so close to hers.

The scent of him infused her head and half dizzied her senses. She not only felt incredibly safe, but his nearness stirred up her physical desire for the man.

They stopped walking in front of the grocery store where the owner, Howard Griffen, was serving up pulled pork sandwiches and French fries at a reasonable price.

"Sound good?" Jacque asked her.

"Smells delicious," she replied.

"Heck yes, they smell delicious, and they taste even better," Howard said. "Should I serve you up a couple with fries on the side?"

"Yeah, that would be great," Jacque replied.

Minutes later, Monique held the two plates while Jacque once again pulled her tight against his side. They returned to the shop and ate while Samantha left to go get some food.

The rest of the day passed with sales made and plenty of laughter as friends and neighbors stopped by. Dominique came and bought a scarf and told them Angelique was keeping busy at her sidewalk sale. Nola also showed up, more to gossip than to buy anything.

At five o'clock, as they began to move things inside, a layer of clouds moved in, darkening the day. "I hope it isn't going to rain," Monique said. "That would certainly ruin everyone's fun."

"The weather report called for a cloudy evening, but it's not supposed to rain," Jacque replied.

"That's good," she said and then turned to Samantha. "You're officially off duty. Thank you so much for working with me today."

Samantha smiled. "I really enjoyed it, and I'll see you day after tomorrow when I work again." She got her purse from inside the store, then with goodbyes said, headed down the sidewalk.

Finally, everything was put away in the store. Monique and Jacque stepped back outside, and she locked the door and then gazed down the street. All the shoppers had disappeared, leaving the sidewalks relatively empty. She knew most of the people were either by the bandstand or enjoying the small carnival that had set up in a field just behind City Hall.

"With the cloudy skies, the lights of the carnival really sparkle and shine," she said. "Especially the ones on the Ferris wheel."

"I suppose you want me to ride it with you," Jacque said from behind her.

She whirled around to look at him. "Would you?"

"I suppose I could do one ride."

"Oh, thank you, Jacque." On impulse she stood on her tiptoes and threw her arms around his neck. She kissed him on his cheek as once again she smelled the delicious scent of him. Instantly, a familiar flame flickered to life inside her.

She quickly lowered her arms, but not before she saw the flames that danced in the depths of his green eyes. "Let's go," she said with a forced lightness.

As usual, as they made their way down the sidewalk, he tucked her into the shelter of his arm. This nearness further stoked the flames that burned in her veins.

She wanted him. In spite of his bouts of coolness, despite his occasional gruffness, she wanted her body naked against his and his hot mouth consuming hers. She wanted to feel him caress her, and she wanted to run her hands across his broad chest and down his perfect body.

She tried to tamp down these emotions. What happened to just wanting him as a friend? Maybe they could be friends with benefits. That would be absolutely perfect. She could have his friendship and his body.

By the time they reached the line for the Ferris wheel, she had successfully managed to shove her desire for Jacque to the back of her head.

They didn't speak as they waited for their turn to get on the big wheel. He kept his arm around her, and she was aware of his gaze going to the left and right of them. Her bodyguard was on duty.

They were next in line when George Trahan approached them. It was fairly obvious he had been drinking throughout the day.

"Hey, Jacque… Monique." He offered them a loopy grin as he slurred his words. "Monique, it's so good to see you up and around."

"Thanks, George," she replied.

"I was so damn sorry when I heard what happened to you. You three sisters have really had a rough time lately," he said. "Is Daniel hot on the trail of who beat you up?"

"He's working the case and eager to find the person responsible," she replied.

"So how long do you think you'll be staying in my man's shanty?" He clapped Jacque on the back. "Or are you two a real romantic couple now?"

"No, it's not like that," she replied quickly. "Jacque is a good friend just helping me out until I completely heal."

"And she's going to be with me for quite a while," Jacque added firmly.

Then it was time for them to slide into one of the Ferris wheel's benches, and George wandered away. The safety bar clicked into place, and then they were lifted up so the rest of the seats could be filled.

Up and up they went. "Look, you can see the swamp from here," she said when they reached the very top. She grabbed hold of his hand in excitement. "And you can see the whole town."

She turned to look at him. The bright reds and blues and yellows of the lights flashed on his features. "It's beautiful, isn't it?"

His eyes glowed with neon green flames, and the fire there had nothing to do with the carnival lights. They were on the top of the world when his lips took hers.

THE KISS ONLY lasted a minute. Still, it was long enough to shoot hot desire through his body. It was enough to make him realize just how badly he wanted her.

When he drew back from her, he released a forced small laugh. "Chalk that up to carnival madness," he said. He'd not been able to stop himself from kissing her. She'd looked so beautiful with the lights of the carnival coloring her features and her eyes glittering so brightly.

Her gaze held his. It was so soft…so inviting. "I like a little carnival madness in my day."

"You'd better enjoy the view because this ride won't last forever," he replied as he released her hand.

Around and around they went, but all too quickly, the ride came to an end. "Is there anything else you want to do?" he asked. Although this whole carnival thing wasn't his cup of tea, he wanted to make sure she had a good time. She deserved it after all she'd been through.

"I think I'm ready to go home," she said.

"Why don't we grab a hot dog to eat before we leave

so we don't have to worry about making dinner?" he suggested.

"Sure, that sounds good to me," she agreed.

It didn't take long for them to find a vendor who was selling grilled hot dogs. He got her one and he got two for himself. They both got chips and a drink. Directly in front of the vendor was a picnic table so they both sat to eat.

The music from the band was audible, and a light breeze made it a pleasant evening. He tried not to look at Monique. He was particularly vulnerable to her loveliness tonight.

She was in a pink two-piece outfit that heightened the silky fall of her dark hair and her medium skin tone. The makeup she wore was just enough to enhance the pink of blush on her cheeks and her eyelashes were darkened with mascara even though he didn't think she needed it.

There had been far too much closeness between them all day long. Her scent had invaded all his senses and the warmth of her body when he pulled her against his side had stirred him to the very depths of his soul.

They finished eating and then headed back to All That Jazz where his car was parked. Once they were in the car, all he could think about was his need to distance himself from her. The sweetness of the kiss still lingered on his lips, a guilty pleasure for sure.

"Did you have fun today?" he asked as he pulled out on Main Street.

"I had a lot of fun," she replied. He felt her gaze on him, but he kept looking at the road. "Thank you, Jacque."

That made him cast her a quick glance. "Thank you for what?"

"Oh, where do I begin?" she said with the light tone he loved to hear. "Thank you for spending your entire day at the dress shop and for protecting me. I also appreciate you smiling at the customers who came by. Thank you also for the Ferris wheel ride."

"Smiling was a tough job, but I managed to summon up a few, so I didn't scare all the women away," he replied. All he wanted to do now was get home and distance himself as much as possible from her.

He was grateful that the day had been a success for her business, and he was glad she was happy. He liked seeing her happy. Thankfully nobody had come after her with ill intent, and for now all was right in the world.

"Are you tired?" he asked and shot another quick look her way.

She caught his gaze and smiled. "Not really. In fact, I still feel rather energized by the day. What about you?"

"I'm a bit tired," he replied. It wasn't true. He was energized as well. But the best thing he could do was go straight to bed as soon as they got home.

It was seven thirty, and a false darkness had fallen due to the cloudy skies. It was a perfect night for an early bedtime, and hopefully by morning he would be able to put away the fierce desire that had simmered through him the entire day.

They reached his shanty, and the first thing he did was turn on several of the lanterns in the room. He then unfastened his holster and set it and his gun in his bedside table.

Monique slung her purse onto the sofa, but she didn't sit down.

"I think I'm going to head on to bed," he said.

She walked over to where he stood and stopped just in front of him. Instantly her body heat wafted toward him, along with the heady scent of her. Tension tightened his stomach. Flames fired through him as he waited for her to speak.

"Jacque," she whispered his name as her eyes lit with a light that could only be a wealth of desire. "I want you."

Those three words dizzied his brain. Somewhere in the back of his mind, he knew he should step back from her. But he remained frozen in place as he felt himself drowning in the desire he'd felt for her for so long.

She reached out and took his hand. "Jacque, I know you want me, and I want you so badly." She gave his hand a tug. "Please, come into my bedroom and make love to me."

She took another step toward him and now stood so close to him that her breasts touched his chest and her breath was warm on his neck.

"Kiss me," she said softly. "Jacque, kiss me and then come to my room and let's make love."

Heaven help him, but he could do nothing but comply. His mouth took hers in a fiery kiss that weakened his knees and nearly stole his breath away.

Her lips plied his with a heat that was intoxicating. When she opened her mouth to allow him to deepen the kiss, he did just that, swirling his tongue with hers as a wealth of pleasure rushed through him.

The kiss finally ended, and as if in a daze, he watched as she grabbed one of the lanterns and then he followed her into the bedroom. She set the lantern on the night-stand and turned back to him. Gently he wrapped his arms around her and kissed her once again.

It had been so long. It had been so damn long since he had held a woman in his arms, so damn long since he'd kissed a woman with such fiery desire and intent.

It was another blazing kiss that fully aroused him. She was sweetness and heat as she pressed her body against his, making it impossible for any other thoughts to enter his head. There was just Monique and him and these moments in time.

When the kiss finally ended, she took a step back from him and began unfastening the buttons of her blouse. He mirrored her movements and started unbuttoning his shirt.

As she shrugged off the blouse, and it fell to the floor behind her, his breath caught in the back of his throat at her beauty. Although she was petite, her breasts were full in the wispy white bra she wore.

He shrugged off his shirt and then unbuttoned the fly of his slacks. All he could think of now was holding her naked body against his own.

He kicked off his shoes and took off his socks and his pants, while she took off her sandals and the pink pants she'd worn that day.

Finally, he was in a pair of black boxers and she wore only her bra and a matching pair of wispy panties. As he climbed into the bed with her, the sheets smelled of her scent and her eyes glowed with a wealth of pleasure and the simmer of her desire.

He pulled her back into his arms, reveling in the feel

of her near nakedness against his own. Her skin was so soft and warm, as if fevered by his very touch.

She raised up just enough to unfasten her bra and he plucked it off her and tossed it to the floor. He then covered her breasts with his hands. He ran his thumbs over her erect nipples and then leaned his head down and captured one of them in his mouth.

As he licked and toyed with first one and then the other, she released a deep moan. There was no better sound than a woman's moans when making love. The sound only made his passion burn hotter.

She tangled her fingers in his hair and then swept them down his back. He then ran a hand down the length of her body…down…down until he reached the waistband of her panties.

A small gasp escaped her as he swept his fingers back and forth. "Take them off," she said breathlessly. "And take yours off."

He took off his boxers first and then moved to take off her panties. She raised her hips to aid him, and then they were both completely naked.

Once again, he pulled her tight against him and kissed her. The kiss was wild and hungry as he ran his hand down the length of her small body once again. He tried to be as gentle as possible, recognizing that her ribs weren't fully healed yet.

Their legs tangled together, and he loved the feel of her soft skin against his. "You are so beautiful," he murmured.

"So are you," she replied half breathlessly.

The foreplay went on until he could no longer stand it.

She gasped once again as his hand slowly slid down

to the very center of her. He began to move his fingers against her moistness. Slowly at first and then faster and faster.

She writhed against him as she moaned his name. Her hips rose up to meet him, and he could feel the tension rising up inside her. Then she was there, and she clung to him as she trembled with her release.

After it was over, she reached down and took him in her hand as her eyes sparkled brightly. She moved her hand up and down the hard length of him, and he couldn't help but hiss with pleasure.

In fact, it was a pleasure so great it threatened to completely undo him. After only a minute or two of her ministrations, he pushed her hand away, but instead of rolling on top of her, ever mindful of her ribs, he picked her up and placed her on top of him.

She straddled him and once again he was struck by her absolute beauty. The glow of the lantern played on her delicate features. She leaned forward and her hair fell down on either side of her face. The silky strands brushed against his chest, further intensifying the heat inside him.

Finally, when he was at a fever pitch, she slowly lowered herself onto him. Sweet heat surrounded him as she held him tightly inside. He grabbed her low on her hips to aid her as she began to move up and down. Oh, he was in a sensual bliss that made him utterly senseless. He moved his hips to meet her thrusts as they came faster and faster.

She moaned, and he answered it with a groan of his own. She then shuddered with another orgasm, and he found his own. He stiffened against her as wave after wave of intense pleasure swept through him.

They remained still for several long moments and then she rolled off onto the side of him. "That was the very best carnival ride to end the day with," she said softly.

He couldn't help but laugh. "You are a silly woman," he replied. He turned his head to gaze at her and was unsurprised to find her smiling. "Actually, I hope I didn't hurt you."

"No, you were very gentle and utterly fantastic," she replied as her eyes glowed with warmth.

"You weren't so bad yourself." He broke his gaze from her, a need to escape suddenly rising up inside him. "I think it's time I head into my own room."

"If you want, you could sleep here with me," she replied. Her voice was soft once again, and he believed he heard a longing there.

He had already broken every rule he'd set for himself by making love with her. There was no way he would further his offenses with the intimacy of falling asleep with her in his arms.

"Thanks for the invite, but I'd rather sleep in my own bed." He got out of the bed, aware of her intense gaze on him as he gathered his clothing from around the floor. When he had it all in hand, he smiled at her. "Since tomorrow is your day off, maybe we can do a little fishing together."

"That sounds like fun," she agreed.

"Then I'll just say good night, and I'll see you in the morning."

It took him only a couple minutes in the bathroom to clean up and then he went into his room and got into bed. He heard her go into the bathroom and then back to her room,

The shanty was silent. The perfect time for self-recriminations, and he had plenty. Making love with Monique had been magical, but it was something he'd never wanted to do. Hell, he hadn't even wanted to kiss her.

However, tonight he had been helpless to contain his emotions. The weeks of desire he'd felt toward her had peaked and exploded to the point where he could do nothing other than make love with her.

He'd promised himself he would never care about a woman again, but his feelings for Monique were growing complex, confusing and more than a little bit frightening. Somehow, someway, he needed to shut them down.

Chapter Ten

She was in love with Jacque LeBlanc. That was Monique's very first conscious thought when she awakened the next morning. A blossom of sweet warmth opened up in her chest at the realization. It both thrilled her and frightened her more than just a little bit.

Falling in love certainly hadn't been in her plans, but in this moment, she was utterly filled with it. Somehow the swamp loner who was more apt to scowl than to smile had crawled deep within her heart, straight into her very soul.

Making love with him the night before had definitely been magical and beyond wonderful. He'd been so gentle and yet so very passionate. Even now her body was warm from the memory of his caresses. Still, despite the sexual explosion that had taken place the night before, she really had no idea what Jacque felt about her.

Oh, she knew he wanted her, but beyond that she had no idea what his feelings were for her. He blew so hot and cold, and she never knew what kind of mood she would get from him. Maybe he was destined to be her very first heartbreak. Didn't every woman have one?

Before this depressing thought could gain any real purchase in her mind, she got out of bed.

She dressed in a bright yellow sundress, knowing from the weather report that it was supposed to be a hot day. Autumn would soon be approaching, her mother's favorite season. That was when the stifling temperatures grew more pleasant, and the greens looked greener, and the yellows appeared brighter.

Monique sat on the edge of her bed as thoughts of her mother momentarily overwhelmed her. She had been so desperate to find the murderer, and that desperation still lived deep inside her.

She was just waiting for a better idea to strike so she could continue hunting the killer. Of course, she didn't intend to say anything to Jacque until she was ready with that kind of a plan. With her body healing up nicely, thoughts of catching the murderer and the person who had beaten her were more and more on her mind again.

But right now, she was ready to go out and see Jacque. Were things going to be awkward between them this morning after the night they had shared?

There was only one way to find out. She got up from the bed and left the room. As with most mornings, Jacque sat at the kitchen table with a cup of coffee before him. At her appearance, he gazed at her and smiled. The smile put her nerves at ease.

"Good morning," he said.

"And a good morning to you," she replied brightly. She got herself a cup of coffee and then joined him at the table.

"How did you sleep?" he asked.

"Like a baby. What about you?" She took a tentative sip of the hot brew.

"Same," he replied. "I thought after lunch we could go out back and do a little fishing."

"That sounds really exciting. I've never fished before," she replied.

He looked at her in obvious surprise. "Never? You grew up in the swamp, and you've never been fishing?"

"Never. Mama paid some of the men in the swamp to keep us supplied in fish for meals, but us girls were never allowed to fish. It was one of her rules I never really understood. I think maybe she was afraid we'd fall off the bank and get eaten by a gator." She was grateful that there was no awkwardness between them this morning.

"Then this afternoon I'll make sure you learn to fish like a pro," he said. "And I'll even keep you from being eaten by a gator."

She laughed. "Thanks, I appreciate that. I'm also feeling a bit of a challenge coming on. You teach me, and I'll pull in more fish than you."

"Ha!" His eyes lit up. "Challenge accepted. Let's say if I win, then you have to cook the fish for dinner tonight."

"Fine, and if I win, then we have a dance party in the living room. Just you and me, dancing to some fun music." She'd missed dancing. It had been such a part of her life before her mother's murder...before her sisters had found love.

"Great, but I'm not dusting off my dancing shoes just yet," he said with a sparkle in his eyes. "Hmm, I can just taste the fish you're going to cook up for dinner."

She laughed. "You're a jerk."

"Maybe a little," he agreed. "Now, let's talk about what we want for breakfast."

The morning passed pleasantly. They small-talked

off and on, and in between he read and she played on her phone. After a lunch of sandwiches and chips, they went out the back door where he handed her one of the fishing poles that leaned against the shanty.

The afternoon sun was warm but a slight breeze kept it pleasant. He led her down a path away from his shanty and to his fishing hole. "Wow, nothing like having a great place like this right outside your back door," she said. It was a fairly large pond of water. Trees lined it, offering both shade and beauty as they rose up majestically.

"It is nice," he agreed.

"I guess you've missed a lot of fishing while I've been here." She looked up at him.

"Not so much. I've managed to get in a little fishing while you are at work."

"That's good. I know my presence here has disrupted your life, and you hate that."

"You haven't really disrupted my life," he said with a wry smile that belied his words. "Now, the first rule of fishing is learning to bait your own hook." He set down the tackle box he carried and then opened a container that held big, fat earthworms. "Watch while I bait mine, and then you can bait yours."

"Yucky," she said as he pulled out a big fat worm and then threaded it on his hook.

"Now, your turn."

"Double yucky." She managed to successfully bait her hook, and then he showed her how to cast the line out. It took her three times of trying before she managed to get the line far enough away from the shore and into the deeper water.

"Now we sit and wait for a bite." He sank down to the grassy bank, and she did as well.

"It's very peaceful here," she observed after a couple of minutes.

"Yeah, I find a lot of my peace here."

They sat in a comfortable silence for a little while. Birds sang merry songs from the tops of the trees, and small animals could be heard rustling through the brush behind them. There was a sort of primeval hush here that was very appealing.

He must have showered before she'd gotten up that morning. They sat close enough together that she could smell the minty scent of his soap and the ocean breeze fragrance of his shampoo. That all mingled with the aroma of shaving cream and his cologne. It made her realize that despite making love with him the night before, she wanted him all over again. She'd never, ever felt this way about a man before.

"I didn't use a condom last night," he said, breaking the silence and surprising her with the topic. "Hell, I don't even have any condoms."

"It's okay. I take birth control pills, and I don't believe you're a promiscuous man," she replied. "And I'm not a promiscuous woman, so we should be safe."

"You know it was a mistake." He continued to gaze straight ahead across the water. "We should have never gone there, and I definitely won't go there again."

"I don't understand why it was such a big mistake? Both of us are consenting adults and don't have significant others."

He turned and looked at her, his gaze dark and shuttered against her. "You don't have to understand. I just need you to know that I won't allow myself again to lose control like I did last night." His gaze returned to the water.

"So noted." She couldn't help but feel a little hurt by his words, especially since she didn't comprehend his issues. Once again, she felt as if Jacque had inner demons. They were demons that had made him choose a shanty in the swamp and a life without laughter, without joy and without love.

"Oh, I think I've got one," she exclaimed as the tip of her pole bent down.

"Give it a small jerk to set the hook," he said. "And then reel it in."

She did as he instructed and then got to her feet and reeled. She cried out in triumph as she landed a nice-size catfish.

Thankfully, he removed the fish from the hook for her and then put it into a basket that floated in the water. "I believe that's one for me and zero for you," she teased.

"Don't get cocky, there's plenty more time left for me to catch up to you," he said with a laugh.

They fished for about two hours and then called it a day. She had three fish in the basket, and he had two. "You'd better start looking for those dancing shoes," she said with a grin as they started the walk back to his shanty.

"It must have been beginner's luck. Either that or you had an amazing teacher," he cassid.

"Ha, don't make excuses. I just fished way better than you today," she teased.

"I demand a rematch on another day."

She laughed. "You're obviously a glutton for punishment because I'll just beat you again."

They were almost to the back door when the shot rang out. The bullet whizzed precariously close to her head. She screamed in terror.

"Get down," Jacque cried out. He grabbed her hand and pulled her to the ground with his body covering hers.

He yanked his gun from his holster and pointed it to the right, where he believed the shooter was somewhere hiding in the bushes. Even with all his muscles tensed and with him filled with a wealth of adrenaline, he could still feel Monique trembling with fear beneath him.

Damn, where was the shooter hiding and was he going to fire again? Right now, with him shielding her, there was no way she could get shot. But there was no question that the bullet had been meant for her.

If she'd been a mere inch to the left, it would have found its mark in her head. The very idea squeezed his chest tight. Death had come far too close to her.

Seconds ticked by…then minutes, and no other bullets flew. Finally enough time had passed that he believed the imminent danger was over. He half rose from his prone position. Nothing happened.

Still, he wasn't willing to take a chance with Monique's life. He glanced down at her. She was on her back beneath him, and her eyes were wide with fear and full of tears.

"We're close enough to the back door that we should be able to crawl inside. I'll raise up some more, and you turn over so you can crawl. Once you get inside, stay away from all of the windows."

She nodded, and within minutes they were safely inside the shanty. He closed and locked the door and then stared out the window for several long minutes. Seeing nothing amiss, he turned back to her. She had collapsed on the sofa where she still visibly trembled.

"I'm going to call Daniel," he said. Once the call was made, he sank down in his chair.

"That bullet was meant for me," she said faintly. Tears welled up in her eyes. "I… I thought it was over. Since nothing had happened for so long, I really thought the danger was over." Her tears spilled down her cheeks as she began to cry in earnest.

He didn't want to touch her, he definitely didn't want to hold her close to him. But there was no way he could just sit in his chair and watch her weep. She'd had a terrible scare, and it was no wonder she was crying.

He got out of his chair and sat down next to her on the sofa. He couldn't help but pull her into his arms.

She leaned into him and cried into the front of his shirt while he stroked up and down her back in an effort to sooth her.

She didn't cry for long, and then she leaned back from him and wiped the last of the tears from her cheeks. "I… I'm sorry. I…just… It's not every day I get shot at."

"There's no reason to apologize for being scared. Hell, I was scared," he replied. He got up from the sofa and returned to his chair.

"I really believed the killer was done attacking me," she said.

"I was beginning to believe you were safe, too," he admitted. It was true. As time had gone by and nothing had happened to give him pause, he'd assumed the killer had gone back underground and was no longer worried about Monique. He'd even started to think about her going back to her own shanty. But now that certainly wasn't going to happen any time soon.

"How did anyone even know we'd be out back fishing today?" she asked.

"I can only guess that once again somebody has been eavesdropping at my windows." Perhaps George Trahan? He'd been caught once before at the back of the shanty. Or was it somebody else altogether?

"I've completely changed my mind. I now believe the killer lives here in the swamp," he said.

"That's even more frightening than him being from town. That means I may know the killer fairly well." Her chocolate-colored eyes flashed with a combination of fear and confusion. "We were so focused on the killer being from town and now we need to rethink everything."

"We don't need to rethink anything. We need to leave things up to Daniel and his men now," he replied firmly. A knock sounded on his door. "And that should be him now." He got up from the chair and went to answer the door.

It was Daniel and four of his men. Jacque ushered them all inside and then told them about coming back to the shanty after fishing and the gunshot that had dropped them in their path.

"Is it possible the shot was an errant one from a hunter in the area?" Clay Caldwell, one of Daniel's right-hand men asked.

"Impossible," Jacque replied quickly. "Nobody ever

hunts that close to a shanty, and that bullet was definitely directed at Monique's head."

"Why, Monique? You have to know some reason why somebody wants you dead." Daniel gazed at her with a pointed intensity. "Someone beat the hell out of you, and now this… You have to have a clue about what's going on."

Monique was still for a long moment, and then she released a deep sigh. "It's Mama's killer." To Jacque's surprise, she told him everything. She explained to him about going into people's homes on the ruse of getting book donations for Jacque and then her snooping around for her mother's missing client book.

When she was finished, Daniel turned his angry attention to Jacque. "And you were a part of this, Jacque? You couldn't find some way to stop her?"

"Believe me, I tried to stop her. But when I realized she was going to do it with or without me, I went along in hopes of protecting her from any harm."

Daniel turned his attention back to Monique. "I swear, you Santori women are going to be the very death of me," he exclaimed. "No more investigating on your own, got it? If I get word that you're doing anything like that, I swear I'll lock you up to keep you safe . A lot of things now make sense. Stay out of the investigation."

"Trust me, I'm done. But it's too late, because the killer wants me dead," she replied in obvious misery.

"I'll keep her safe here, and you find the killer," Jacque said.

"Now on that note why don't you take me outside, and we'll see if we can find any kind of evidence. Maybe he dropped something or at least left us a shell casing."

The officers followed Jacque out the back door, and he pointed to where he thought the shooter had been located. "There's a narrow path that leads around this pond. If you follow that, it will take you to the area where I believe the shooter was," Jacque explained as he pointed to a spot across the pond. "I'd go with you, but right now I'm not leaving Monique."

"Understood," Daniel replied and then instructed his men to follow the path while he and Jacque went back inside the shanty. Jacque gestured for Daniel to sit on the sofa with Monique.

"Now the note that was in the box left on your doorstep the night of your beating makes much more sense," Daniel said. "You should have come to me with everything that night."

"I was hoping I would never have to come clean about what I was doing," she replied. "I just wanted… I needed to find the killer."

"For what it's worth, I now believe the killer is definitely from the swamp," Jacque said. He then went on to explain how he believed the killer had to have eavesdropped at his windows. "That's how he knew what Monique and I were doing with the book donation scheme and that we would be fishing this afternoon."

The idea that somebody had been sneaking around his house and listening to their conversations filled Jacque with a wealth of anger. From now on his windows in the kitchen would be closed. It might make the shanty a little stuffy, but nobody would be able to hear any more of their conversations again.

"You might want to check out George Trahan again.

I caught him snooping around the back of my house not too long ago," he said to Daniel.

"Anyone else you consider a suspect?" Daniel looked first at Jacque and then at Monique.

A frown danced in the center of her forehead. "I need time to think about it. I was so certain the killer was somebody prominent in town, but after this attack today everything has changed."

"Your sister isn't going to be pleased by what you've been doing," Daniel said.

"Oh Lordy, Daniel, do you really have to tell her?" She looked miserable. "I would appreciate it if all this could stay with the three of us. Surely you don't want to cause a fight between me and my sisters."

"I guess she doesn't have to know about your previous actions," Daniel conceded.

"Thank you," Monique replied with obvious gratitude.

They all fell silent, and Daniel got up and moved to stand at the back door. Monique looked small and vulnerable as she leaned into the corner of the couch.

As Jacque thought of how close the bullet had come to her head, his heart nearly stopped beating. He had started to believe she was safe from harm, but obviously he'd been very wrong.

Whoever the killer was, he'd marked her for death even though she was done with her snooping. Why? Who could be so threatened by her? Who the hell was this person? How was law enforcement ever going to catch him? These thoughts continued to cascade through his mind.

Time ticked by, and finally the four lawmen returned to the shanty. "We found an area where the grass was tamped down," Luke began. "We believe that's where the shooter waited."

"By the grass pattern, we also believe the shooter was there for a while," Clay added.

"That's probably because we didn't have an exact time that we were going fishing. If the bastard was listening at my window, all he heard was we were going to fish after lunch," Jacque said angrily. "This creep has to be somebody in the swamp. Somebody from town would be noticed if they came all the way into my shanty. I wonder why he waited to shoot until we were almost back here."

"If you were sitting on the bank to fish, then he didn't have a great shot from where he hid until you got closer to the shanty where the ground is a little higher," Clay said. "And unfortunately, we found nothing in the grass that could be used as evidence," Clay said.

Daniel frowned. "I now think you're right about the killer being from the swamp, and that's where we'll intensify our efforts once again. In the meantime, I hope Monique will remain safe here."

"She's not going anywhere," Jacque said firmly.

"We had several men from the swamp on our initial suspect list. We'll now look at those men more closely," Daniel said.

"Can you tell me who was on that list?" Jacque asked. "I'd like to know so I can be aware of them."

Daniel nodded. "Pierre Guidry is one. Maybe we need to sweat Lucien Rousseau and see if he lied to us when he alibied Pierre. Then there's Louis Theriot. We know he was seeing Mystique just before her murder, but we don't know why. Finally, we had Bill Stanger on our list of suspects."

Two of the three were men who came here for reading lessons. Had Jacque invited the killer into his home? Had the killer come inside to see what weakness in Monique's security he might be able to exploit? His blood ran cold at the very thought.

"Me and my sisters always believed Pierre killed our mother in a fit of jealous rage," Monique said. "Of course, that was before Lucien insisted he saw Pierre fishing in the swamp at the time of the murder."

"Monique, I know you've heard this a million times from me, but we're going to get this guy. Now that we know where to focus our investigation, I'm hoping it won't be too much longer now," Daniel said.

Monique gave him a wan smile. "I know you're doing the best you can, and I appreciate all your efforts."

Minutes later the lawmen were gone, and Jacque was once again alone with Monique. She remained curled up and with her gaze at some point over his head. He hated to see her so beaten down…so frightened.

"There are some positive things," he finally said, breaking the silence that had built up in the air.

She turned her gaze to him. Her eyes without their normal sparkle nearly broke his heart. "What kind of positive things?"

"Well, for one thing the bullet missed you. Second, you beat me at fishing. And third, that means we're having a dance party after dinner."

The last thing he wanted to do was dance, but she'd earned it, and she needed something to put the sparkle back in her eyes. He definitely didn't want to begin to examine why her happiness was so damn important to him.

"Right now, I don't feel much like dancing," she replied.

"Maybe you'll change your mind when the time comes."

"We'll see," she replied and then released a deep sigh. "I was really beginning to feel safe again. I thought it was all over, and I would be able to go home and give you your life back."

He smiled at her. "Trust me, my life was nothing special before you started staying here. Besides, I do enjoy your company."

"Just not all the time," she replied and this time a tiny sparkle was back in her eyes. "Trust me, I know there are times you just want me to shut up."

He laughed. "Maybe just occasionally."

"Honestly, Jacque, I don't know what I'd do without you. I… I can never thank you enough for your kindness and protection. I'm just sorry I got you into this whole mess."

"You didn't get me into this mess, and I'm glad I can be here for you," he replied.

It was at that moment Jacque realized the depth of his feelings for her.

He couldn't be in love with her. He'd refused to ever do love again. But his feelings for her felt like love and that scared the hell out of him.

Chapter Eleven

She had almost told him she was in love with him. The words had burned on the tip of her tongue begging to be freed, but thankfully she'd managed to swallow them back.

Now wasn't the time for her to profess her love. With the shooting just now, she had a feeling he would believe it was all about gratitude and fear and not about real love.

She would wait until the time was perfect. And she was hoping when she did confess, he would realize he was in love with her, too. That would be positively wonderful… if it happened that way.

Monique took her phone and went into the bedroom where she called Angelique and then Dominique. The calls were just friendly check-ins. She didn't mention her close call with a bullet. The last thing she wanted to do was worry them. They both had wonderful lives, doing what they wanted for work and living with the men who loved them. There was no reason to bring her drama to them, although she had no idea if Daniel actually would tell Angelique about the shooting.

After that she called the store and had a quick con-versation with Cynthia who was working. Cynthia indicated that everything was fine although it had been a slow sales day.

With all the shock of the shooting, Monique needed a little normalcy and talking to her sisters and checking in at the store gave her that for a moment. She finally left the bedroom and returned to the living room. Jacque wasn't there.

She found him on the back porch, cleaning the fish they had caught. "Don't come out here," he said when he saw her. "I'm almost finished, and then I'll be back in."

She turned around and headed to her usual spot on the sofa. He came in just a few minutes later, a pan of fish fillets in his hand. "Are you hungry?" he asked.

"I guess I could eat." She looked at the time on her phone, surprised to realize it was almost six thirty. With the shooting, the day had completely slipped away.

"Sit tight, and I'll have some fish fried up and a salad made in just a few minutes," he replied.

She got up and moved from the sofa to the kitchen table to watch him cook.

"If I had caught two more fish, you would be in here fixing dinner." He cast her a quick smile. "If you feel like it after dinner, I'm ready for a dance party. We need a little fun around here."

"Jacque LeBlanc is looking for some fun? Wow, I'm impressed, and I'm definitely up for some fun, too," she replied. "I used to love dancing at the Voodoo Lounge. Usually from the minute we got there until we went home, I was out on the dance floor the whole time."

"I've never been there," he said as he dredged the fish through a flour mixture and then put the pieces in the awaiting skillet.

"You would probably hate it. It's loud and usually really crowded. Besides, you've never been to most of the places in town," she replied dryly. "It wouldn't be seemly for the town's hermit to be seen out and about."

"Hey, I was out and about with you," he protested. "And I resent being called a hermit." His eyes twinkled with a teasing light.

"Okay then, a curmudgeon, a cranky-pants, an ogre…"

"I refuse to wear any of those titles when I was just a loner minding my own business before a beautiful woman knocked on my door and turned my world upside down."

"Just think how bored you would be if that woman hadn't knocked on your door," she replied.

"True, my life would be boring without you," he agreed.

She knew he was trying to put her in a good mood, despite what had happened earlier in the day, and she really appreciated his efforts. They only made her love him more.

By the time they finished eating, it was almost seven thirty, and she was actually looking forward to a little dancing to end the night. She was definitely interested to see how Jacque might move to some music.

They turned on the lanterns around the room, and then she told him what station to set his phone to for the best oldies music.

Finally, they began to dance. To her surprise, Jacque showed perfect rhythm and was remarkably light on his feet. It wasn't long before they were laughing together as they fell into a contest of who could dance sillier.

She couldn't have loved him anymore than she did

in these moments. He was everything she wanted in a partner…in a lover and in a husband.

A million times during the evening she had to fight against the desire to tell him how she felt. If she spoke it aloud, and he told her he didn't love her, then things would be awkward between them. That was the last thing she wanted, especially since she didn't know how long she'd be here with him.

They finally collapsed on the sofa to catch their breaths, and he turned his phone volume down.

"You're a very good dancer," she said.

"I haven't danced in years," he replied. "I guess it's kind of like riding a bicycle. Once you learn how to do it, it always comes back to you."

"I wouldn't know about that, I've never ridden a bicycle," she replied.

"You haven't missed much," he replied. He turned his phone off, indicating that the dance party was over. She was good with that. They had been dancing for almost an hour, and suddenly she was utterly exhausted.

It now felt as if the day had been extremely long. It seemed like ages ago that somebody had tried to kill her. She said her good night to Jacque and then went into her bedroom.

As tired as she was, once she was in bed, her mind refused to shut off. Somebody wanted her dead.

And she knew all the suspects Daniel had named. She didn't know them well, but they'd always exchanged friendly smiles when she'd encountered them in the swamp. And now one of them wanted her dead. Who was it? Who had killed her mother and was now after her? Dammit, who was it?

Then there were her feelings for Jacque. At least those weren't confusing at all. She definitely hadn't been looking for love, but she had found it with Jacque. He'd proven to be a man of many layers, and she still believed there were things about him she didn't know…things that occasionally had him withdrawn and miserable. The sexual tension was still very hot between them, but she couldn't forget that he'd told her he would never make love to her again.

No, she wasn't confused about her feelings for him, but she was definitely confused about his feelings toward her.

She finally fell asleep and awakened the next morning just after dawn. She got up and pulled on her robe with the intent of taking a shower. She had to be at work at nine, but she had plenty of time to shower, dress and eat breakfast.

Jacque was at the kitchen table and greeted her with a smile. "I'll go get you a towel," he said.

"Sit tight, I know where they are." She stepped into the bathroom where the towels were neatly folded on a shelf in a closet. She grabbed one and then returned to the kitchen.

Thankfully the shower was made of wood and nobody would be able to see her inside, so she should be safe. "I'll be right back in." She opened the back door and immediately stepped into the shower stall.

It didn't take long for her to shower and wash her hair. When she was finished, she went back to her bedroom to get dressed for the day and brush out her wet hair. When that was done, she returned to the kitchen, poured herself a cup of coffee and then sat at the table.

Jacque stood in front of the stovetop, tending frying bacon. "Bacon and eggs okay?" he asked.

"Fine with me," she agreed. "So what are your plans while I'm at work today?"

"I think I'm going to take a stroll around the swamp, see what kind of scuttlebutt I can pick up."

"Oh, Jacque, please don't stir things up," she said as fear leaped into her throat. "The last thing we want is for the killer to come after you, too."

"Trust me, I'm not going to get myself into any trouble." He took the bacon out of the skillet and then whipped up a bowl full of eggs, milk and cheese. She watched him as he drained the grease from the skillet into a tin can and then added the eggs to cook.

He turned to look at her. "Don't look so worried, Monique. I'm just going to take a bit of a walk and visit with some people. Who knows, maybe I'll get lucky and find out some information about who shot at you yesterday." He turned his attention back to the skillet.

"So far luck hasn't exactly been on our side," she said dryly.

"Maybe that will change today," he replied.

An hour later she was in the shop waiting for customers to come in. While she waited, she worried about the man she loved. She didn't like the idea of him being out and about where the killer might be. He might ask the wrong question to the wrong person.

What was to stop the perpetrator from murdering him? That would then leave her vulnerable and easy to kill. But that wasn't the worst thing. If Jacque got killed, she would be responsible and would mourn his death for the rest of her life. Her heart cringed at the very thought of losing him.

He'd been living a peaceful, solitary life before she'd gotten him involved in all this. She would never forgive herself if something bad happened to him.

The hours at the shop passed quickly as she was busy for most of the day. At two o'clock, she breathed a sigh of relief at the sight of his car pulled against the curb.

"Cynthia, my ride is here, so I'll see you tomorrow," she said to the woman who had arrived minutes before.

"Okay, see you tomorrow, Monique," she answered and then Monique left the shop and slid into Jacque's car.

"Well, you don't look any worse for the wear," she said as she eyed him.

"Did you expect me to show up here with a missing arm or leg after fighting with the killer in the swamp?" he asked in obvious amusement.

"No, that's the way I would expect you to show up after fighting with a big gator in the swamp," she replied. "But it's not funny, Jacque, I've been worried about you all day."

His smile faded, and he put the car into gear. "There's no need to worry about me, Monique. I can take care of myself."

He roared away from the curb. "Well, excuse me for worrying about somebody I consider my best friend," she replied.

He cast her a half smile. "Okay, I forgive you. How was work?"

"Good. It was a fairly busy day, and the time flew by."

"What about your ribs? How do they feel?"

"They're still sore, but the pain is mostly manageable now. So dare I ask, how did your day go?" she asked.

"I had a pretty good day. I did walk around the swamp a bit. I visited for a little while with George and Louis. I looked around for Bill, but he must work at the café today."

"Did you get any helpful information or strange feelings from them?" she asked.

"No, not really. As gator-hunters both George and Louis would have guns, but I don't know if Bill owns a gun or not. As a busboy at the café, he would really have no need to own one."

"But most people who live in the swamp do have guns." She released a deep sigh. "Maybe Daniel will come up with something," she said hopefully.

They fell silent for the rest of the drive home. Once they reached the shanty, she went into her bedroom to change out of the attractive black-and-white dress she'd worn to work. Instead, she pulled on a pair of jeans and a dark green T-shirt. She then went back into the living room where Jacque was seated in his chair.

"How about I make dinner for you tonight?" she suggested. "You're always cooking for me, so it's way past my turn to cook for you."

"Well, that sounds great to me. Feel free to use whatever is in the cooler and my pantry," he replied. "And I'll just sit here and relax."

"Then I'll head into the kitchen and get busy." After she got out the cookstove dand he went out to start the generator, she found three chicken legs and three thighs in the cooler that she decided to fry up.

It was about an hour later when she had everything

ready to serve. The chicken had fried up nice and crispy, and she'd made a ranch macaroni salad that she'd found in the pantry. There was also corn and bread and butter. They small-talked through the meal.

This is what it would be like to be married to him, she thought. They would share the events of their days and would make and eat their meals together. Then they would go to bed together where they would make love and then she would fall asleep in the warmth of his embrace. She wanted that. Oh, she wished for it so badly.

It was around five thirty when the kitchen was clean and they returned to the living room. Her love for him was so full in her chest, it ached.

He had told her many stories about his previous work as a police officer. He'd also shared with her his childhood antics. There seemed to be only one subject they hadn't really talked about in depth.

"Jacque, tell me about your wife," she asked.

He looked up at her. His green eyes were dark, and his features were taut with a sudden tension. "I'll tell you all you need to know about my wife and my four-year-old daughter. I killed them. I killed them both, and that's what ended my marriage."

Jacque saw the horrifying shock on Monique's features. Hell, he had shocked himself by blurting out the words. He'd never spoken about what had happened to Lauren and Lily. Even now thoughts of them caused an enormous pressure in the center of his chest.

Monique's eyes were huge. "Wha…what do you mean?" she asked softly.

He squeezed his eyes tightly closed as memories suddenly cascaded through his mind. He had spent the last four years trying to forget. But now, the memories and the trauma rose up to the surface, and he realized he wanted…needed to talk about it.

"Lauren and I were high school sweethearts," he began. "We got married right after I joined the police force. Almost immediately she got pregnant with our daughter, Lily."

The utter joy of the moment of birth had been something he had never felt before and would never feel again. He and Lauren had laughed and cried together as baby Lily burst into the world.

He opened his eyes and stared at a point just over Monique's head as the pain of his past seared through him, quickly erasing that particular memory of joy.

"Lauren was a high school teacher, but when Lily was born, she quit her job to be a stay-at-home mom, which was fine with me. Lily was the cutest, smartest little girl in the entire world. She loved the color pink and giggling and her mommy and me."

His pain made him half breathless, and tears burned at his eyes as he thought of the woman who had loved him so fiercely and the little girl who had held his heart.

Lily had been a daddy's girl and had believed he was the very bestest daddy in the whole wide world. "When I'd come home stressed from the job, Lily would always put her hands on either side of my face, and she'd tell me to be happy."

He swallowed against his impending tears. "We were so very happy together," he continued. "Lauren was trying to get pregnant again, my job was going well, and Lily was thriving."

He paused a moment as the anguish inside him threatened to overwhelm him. He drew in several deep breaths and then continued.

"It was my birthday, and more than anything I wanted Lauren to bring Lily to have lunch with me at the station. Lauren was tired and really didn't want to come, but I talked her into it."

His heart banged against his ribs as a killing guilt coupled with deep anguish tortured him. He leaned forward and buried his face in his hands. "It was my fault. It was all my fault. If I hadn't insisted that they come to the station, they would still be alive today."

He sensed Monique getting off the couch and coming to kneel beside his recliner. Thank God she didn't touch him, for if he felt her soft, caring touch, he would have completely crumbled.

"I was sitting at my desk inside the police station waiting for them to arrive when I heard the crash outside. It was a horrid sound of twisting metal and breaking glass. Somehow in that moment, I knew they were gone. The drunk driver was a twenty-three-year-old female. They believed she was traveling at a little over seventy miles an hour when she hit Lauren's car head on. Nobody survived."

Nobody survived. When he'd been told that, he had gone wild with grief. His entire world was gone…shattered in a young woman's bad decision to drive drunk and Jacque's selfish desire to see his daughter. "I killed them. If I hadn't insisted on them coming, they would still be alive today."

Monique placed a gentle hand on his shoulder. "Oh, Jacque, I'm so very sorry for your loss." To his surprise, her tender voice soothed some of the raw edges inside of him. "You didn't kill them, Jacque, and you shouldn't burden yourself with that kind of guilt."

He sat back up and gazed at her. Her eyes held a wealth of emotion…sorrow for him, an abundance of care and something else…something that he couldn't quite discern.

"I barely remember the days immediately following the wreck," he admitted. "I was in a black hole, and things only got blacker when it was discovered that at the time of her death Lauren was three and a half months pregnant with a baby boy. I had a feeling she'd intended to tell me the joyous news for my birthday that night after work."

"Oh, Jacque, my heart positively breaks for your loss." Tears filled Monique's eyes and tracked down her cheeks.

He reached out and used his thumbs to wipe away her tears. "Don't cry for me, Monique." His grief slowly eased, as if her tears were washing it away. "This all happened a long time ago, and I've come to terms with it."

"Still, my heart breaks for you," she replied softly. "I can't imagine the pain you've been through, and that hurts me for you because I love you. Jacque, I'm in love with you."

He stared at her in horror. This was the very last thing he'd expected, and it was the very last thing he wanted. For a long moment he was completely speechless.

"Did you hear me, Jacque? I'm madly in love with you, and I believe you are in love with me. If you are, we could build a new happiness together. Jacque, you deserve to be happy again. You deserve love and laughter in your life. Lauren and Lily would want you to be happy again."

"Stop," he snapped. "I don't want to hear anymore." He averted his gaze, unable to look at her. "First of all, I don't do love. I swore to myself when Lauren and Lily died that I would never fall in love again. I want to protect you, and I enjoy your company, but I'm not in love with you."

He looked back at her in time to see her eyes once again well up with tears. "Haven't you punished yourself enough?" she asked softly. "For the last four years, you've punished yourself for a crime you didn't even commit. You didn't kill them, Jacque. A drunk driver killed them, and that driver was the guilty person, not you."

"How could you say you love me? What's to love? I'm a miserable bastard who doesn't deserve love," he replied roughly.

"You are so much more than that," she protested. "Jacque, you are warm and caring, and if you were really just a miserable bastard, I wouldn't love you like I do."

"Stop saying that." Her words of love ached inside him. Especially since he couldn't…wouldn't love her back. To his relief, she got up from the floor next to him and returned to the sofa.

"I… I'm sorry," she said. "I shouldn't have said anything…and I won't speak of it again," she said softly.

God, he'd killed his wife, and now he had hurt Monique. He got up from the chair, needing to get away… needing some time to breathe and recenter himself.

"If you'll excuse me, I'll be back in just a few minutes." He didn't wait for her response, but he went into his bedroom and closed the door behind him. He sank down on the edge of his bed and opened the drawer in his nightstand. He withdrew the framed photo inside and gazed at it.

It had been one of his favorite photos of the two of them. Lauren and Lily had been sitting on their front porch. Their blond hair had sparkled in the sunshine, and they had both been laughing.

They were long gone now, but they would always be sweet memories in his heart. He was surprised to realize that telling Monique about them had helped ease some of his pain.

Logically he knew she was right. He hadn't killed them. The accident could have happened on any day at any time. It was a tragedy, and tragedies happened to a lot of people. He had just never thought it would happen to him.

He was surprised to realize how much healing he had done over the past four years. Time really was a healer of bad things. And Monique, he mentally added.

Her softness and her caring had definitely helped. She was in love with him. Her words of love echoed in his mind and resonated in his heart.

As much as he cared about her, he would never invite her into his life on a permanent basis. She deserved a man who had no real trauma in his life, a man who could love her far better than he could. He would protect her through this storm in her life, and then he'd let her go.

Chapter Twelve

Monique remained on the sofa for several long moments, her heart aching so much she could scarcely move. Tears raced down her cheeks unchecked. Her pain for him and his tragic past mingled with the anguish of now knowing he wasn't in love with her.

She should have never told him how she felt about him. She especially shouldn't have confessed to him her love while he'd been reliving his painful past. Her timing had sucked.

She'd been so sure that he'd been in love with her. He'd shown her his love in a million ways. But apparently, she'd mistaken his emotions.

Now things would definitely be awkward between them. She had burdened him with so much already, and now she had burdened him with her unrequited love.

She needed to talk to somebody. Her emotions were so great inside her that she needed to share them with somebody who could help her make sense of it all.

She didn't want to call her sisters. They were happy in love, and the last thing she wanted to do was encumber them with her problems and love issues. She wished she had a best friend to call, but she didn't. She had considered Jacque to be her best friend.

Now all she wanted was some distance, some time away from him so she could get her thoughts and feelings back under control. She swiped the tears from her eyes and cheeks and then stood.

There was one place she could go where she'd always felt safe, a person she knew she could tell all her troubles to. Surely, she could get there safely as it wasn't that far away.

Jacque would probably be angry that she'd left his shanty alone, but she'd write him a note and let him know where she was. With this thought in mind, she looked in his bookcase until she found a blank notebook. She tore out a page, wrote the note and then left it on the kitchen table.

There was no sound from Jacque's bedroom. Maybe after the explosion of emotions, he'd fallen asleep. There was certainly no reason to awaken him if that was the case.

From her purse on the sofa, she grabbed the knife she carried for self-defense. Of course, it would do no good against a bullet, but hopefully she could sneak through the swamp and get where she was going safely without anyone seeing her.

Tears once again burned at her eyes as she slipped out of the shanty's front door. It was still relatively early so the sun was still up in the sky, although it wouldn't be long before twilight fell.

She immediately stepped into the brush just off the beaten path. She was grateful for the green T-shirt she wore that would help her blend into the landscape.

It was too early for the gator-hunters and fishermen to be out and about, so hopefully she wouldn't encounter anyone. She moved quickly and as silently as possible, staying off the beaten paths as she headed to her destination. Her heart was breaking with each step she took.

She'd had so much hope that she and Jacque could find true happiness together, so much hope that he would realize he loved her as much as she loved him. She'd been so mistaken about him…about his love. How was she going to stop her heart from hurting so badly?

How she wished her mother was here. Her mother would have drawn her into her arms and allowed Monique to cry her eyes out. Then she would have some words of wisdom for her heartbroken daughter. But her mother wasn't here anymore, and this thought made her cry even more.

Aware of the danger that could come at her from any direction, she kept her eyes and ears open as she stifled her sobs. She clutched the knife tightly in her hand, hoping she wouldn't have to use it. But she would if it came to her own survival.

It wasn't long before the little shanty she sought came into view. She ran to the front door and knocked. When the door opened, she burst into tears and collapsed into Nola's familiar arms. Nola was dressed in a blue-flowered housedress, and she smelled of vanilla and childhood love.

"Monique, honey." Nola pulled her into the shanty and then looked beyond Monique's shoulders. "Where's Jacque?" she asked.

"H-he's back at his p-place," Monique replied, tears still falling. "He was in his bedroom when I left. I think he was asleep."

Nola closed the door and then led Monique to her sofa

where she pulled Monique down next to her. "Honey, tell me what's happening. Why are you crying?" She placed an arm around Monique and patted her shoulder. "Did you and Jacque have a fight?"

"No…no fight." Monique replied. She set the knife she'd been carrying down on the coffee table and drew in several deep breaths in an attempt to get her tears under control. "Oh, Nola, I'm so in love with him and he…he doesn't love me back." These words caused a new torrent of tears to fall.

"Oh, honey…are you sure he isn't in love with you?" Nola asked as she continued to hold Monique in her arms.

"P-positive. He told me." Once again Monique attempted to gain control of herself.

"Well, the sad thing is these things happen," Nola replied.

Monique sat up straighter and swiped the tears from her eyes. "I'm sorry… I just… I needed to talk to someone," she said.

"I'm glad you came here. You know you can always talk to me," Nola replied sympathetically.

Monique wound up telling Nola most of her conversation with Jacque, although she didn't tell Nola about the loss of Jacque's wife and child. She knew Nola could be a bit of a gossip, and telling her about that would be a complete betrayal of Jacque's privacy and trust.

Instead, what she spoke about was all the things that had made her fall in love with the handsome loner. She talked about carnival rides and dancing, about long talks and shared laughter. She told Nola about silly jokes and how safe he made her feel, not just physically but emotionally as well. When she finished, she was utterly depleted.

"I'm so sorry, honey," Nola said. "It would be nice if every woman who fell in love with a man would have that love returned tenfold. But sometimes it just doesn't happen that way."

Monique gazed at the woman who had been like a mother to her. "Why have you never married, Nola?"

"Sometimes a broken heart lasts a lifetime," Nola said softly. Her eyes grew distant and hazy as she looked toward the front window. "I was thirty-three when I met the man of my dreams. His name was David, and he was from town and owned a construction company. I was positively crazy about him. He came here two or three nights a week, and we dated for about eight months. I thought for sure we'd eventually get married, and I'd move into town with him and live happily ever after."

She released a deep sigh and looked back at Monique. "But he had bigger plans for himself. When he broke it off with me, he told me his future wasn't in a small swampy town with a swamp woman. Two days after he broke up with me, he picked up and left Dark Waters, and I never heard from him again. I spent months hoping he'd come back for me, praying that he would realize he loved me and couldn't live without me. But of course, that didn't happen."

She grabbed hold of one of Monique's hands. "The whole experience soured me on love. I became a bitter woman and decided I would live the rest of my life alone. Don't be like me, Monique. Don't let this heartache close you off from finding another. You're young and beautiful. There will be another man for you, one you'll love and he'll love you to distraction. You can still have a happily-ever-after ending with another man."

"It's hard to even think about another man right now," Monique replied mournfully.

"Give it time, honey. Like I said, you're young and have your whole life in front of you," Nola said. "Are you going to still remain at Jacque's shanty?"

"Right now, I need to be there," Monique said and then told Nola about being shot at. "I have to stay there for my own safety."

"Good luck navigating that with the way you feel about him," Nola said sympathetically. She released Monique's hand and stood. "Sorry, but right now I need to use the restroom. You just sit tight, and I'll be right back."

As Nola disappeared into the bathroom, Monique got up from the sofa. Her mouth was dry, and she needed something to drink. She knew that Nola often kept a pitcher of iced tea in her cooler.

Nola's shanty had an actual room that served as the kitchen area. It contained a small table and four chairs, a bookcase filled with recipe books and a counter where the cooler sat next to a deep bin that was her sink.

Monique went into the room and walked directly over to the cooler. Sure enough, there was a pitcher of chilled tea inside. She pulled it out and set it on the counter and then opened one of the cabinets to grab a glass. Finally, she settled in one of the chairs at the table with some tea.

Talking to Nola had certainly been cathartic, but it had hardly solved anything. She was still in love with Jacque, and he still wasn't in love with her. She would remain under his protective care, but there was no question that things were going to be awkward and different between them from now on.

In fact, it was probably time for her to head back there now. The only thing she could hope for was that Daniel would solve the crimes sooner rather than later, and she would be able to move back to her own shanty and somehow get over loving Jacque.

For a moment her gaze drifted over the many cookbooks Nola had lined up on the bookshelf next to the table. Nola was a great cook and had often made dinner for Mystique and her three daughters when the girls had been small.

Monique suddenly froze as her heartbeat accelerated with shock. There, tucked between two of the cookbooks, was a very familiar dark blue book.

Her mother's client book.

For just a moment she couldn't make sense of it being there. Nola? Nola had the book? Her brain struggled to make sense of it all. But that meant…oh God, that meant Nola had killed her mother. Nola had beaten Monique and tried to kill her?

She had to get out of here. She needed to tell Jacque. Daniel needed to know. The killer had been identified, and Monique's head whirled with the sickening truth of it. She jerked up out of the chair and put her glass in the sink.

"Monique? Oh, here you are." Nola came into the kitchen.

Act natural, a voice whispered inside Monique's head. *Don't let her know that you saw the book.* "I just came in to get a quick drink of tea." She was grateful that her voice sounded completely normal despite the intense horror that bubbled up inside her.

"I see you found it okay," Nola replied.

Monique forced a smile. "I did. You've always made the best sweet tea. And now it's probably time I head back. If Jacque wakes up, he'll worry that I'm gone."

Together, the two of them walked out of the kitchen. Monique immediately saw that her knife was no longer on the coffee table. It was nowhere in sight.

She started to head for the front door, but Nola got there first. She put her back to the door and frowned at Monique. "You know I can't let you leave here," she said. To Monique's horror, she pulled a long, wicked-looking knife out of her housedress pocket. "There's no need to pretend, honey. I'm sure you saw the book."

For a moment Monique thought about playing dumb, but more than anything and in spite of the danger she knew she was in, she wanted…she needed answers.

"You killed her? Why?" Monique looked at the woman she thought she knew but now realized she didn't know at all. Nola had to be a monster to slice her best friend's throat.

"Your mother was a damned fool," Nola said. There was a hardness in her eyes Monique had never seen before. "That night I came to her with a plan that would have made us both a lot of money, enough money so that I could finally get out of this damn swamp and spend the rest of my life someplace nice."

"What kind of a plan?" Monique mouth had gone dry, and she was torn between the need to understand everything and the desire to scream.

"Your mother knew secrets about a lot of people…

wealthy people who would pay a lot of money to keep those secrets from coming out. The plan I suggested to your mother was that we blackmail her clients. Unfortunately, Mystique didn't see things my way. All the times I cooked meals for her and the three of you…all the times I wiped you and your sisters' snotty noses, and she couldn't do this one thing for me. She knew how much I wanted to get out of the swamp and live an easier life someplace else."

She sneered with obvious disgust. "She told me I was crazy, and she would never do anything like that. Her clients trusted her and blah…blah…blah. I told her I would do it without her, and I tried to grab the client book from her. Anyway, we fought over it, and I killed her and took the book." There was no remorse, no regret at all in her voice. She said the words without any emotion, like she was announcing lunch options.

"But what about me? You left me the notes? You were the one who beat me and tried to shoot me?" Monique felt as if she was in a dream…a nightmare from which she couldn't awaken.

Nola narrowed her eyes. "I had to stop you. I knew you wouldn't stop your digging until you found me out. Out of the three of you girls, you were always the smartest, the most determined, and you were a definite threat to all my plans."

Tears blurred Monique's vision as she continued to stare at the woman. "I… I thought you loved me… I thought you loved all of us."

"Oh, I do. But I love money more. I've been wanting to leave this swamp behind for years, and this is my way to finally get what I want." Nola took a step toward her.

"I intend to lie low for a little while and then I'll start blackmailing the people who will pay me the most money to keep their secrets."

"I could be your partner," Monique said desperately. "Nola, I could work with you, and I swear I wouldn't tell anyone."

Nola laughed. It wasn't the sound of merriment, rather it was the raucous noise of the devil come calling. "Don't be ridiculous," she scoffed. "Ah, Monique, you don't fool me. You're a moral fool just like your mother was."

"Jacque knows I'm here." Monique said urgently and took a step backward. "In fact, he should be here at any time." God, where was he? Was he still in his bedroom, unaware that she was gone? Unaware that she was in danger? Did he just assume she'd be safe here with Nola?

"But he isn't here now, and probably by the time he gets here, you'll be dead in the swamp, attacked by the unknown killer who has been after you. Nobody will ever know you made it here to my shanty." Nola sprang forward, the knife thrusting outward.

Monique screamed and grabbed one of the electric lanterns from an end table. She threw it at the woman, but Nola batted it away like it was nothing, and with another wild burst of laughter, she continued to advance.

Jacque awakened, shocked that he'd actually fallen asleep. He never napped during the day. But he'd never talked about the old trauma before. He'd obviously been overwhelmed by it all. He rolled over on his back and stared up where twilight shadows danced on the ceiling.

It had been such an emotional afternoon, but he felt surprisingly refreshed. Telling Monique about Lauren and Lily had been cathartic. He recognized now that he'd healed a lot in the past four years. His loss of his wife and child would always bring an enormous sadness to him, but it was a sadness now tempered by time and distance.

She loved him.

Monique's words slammed into his chest with a new pain. He shouldn't have been surprised. If he thought about it, he'd seen her love for him in a million ways before she actually spoke the words.

Her eyes had whispered of her love each time she gazed at him. Her smiles had told him how she felt about him. Her simplest touch had spoken of love. When she'd knelt by his side and cried tears for him, it had touched him deeply, and once again had shown her love for him.

He'd been a fool not to have seen it sooner, not to have somehow stopped it from happening. Maybe she was mistaken. He could certainly understand how she might think she was in love with him when actually what she really felt was an enormous amount of gratitude and friendship.

They had been living in such close contact, virtually like husband and wife. He'd been her protector for weeks. Was it any wonder she might mistakenly believe herself to be in love with him?

As for his love for her? He'd get over it. Once this was all over and she moved out of his shanty and went back to her own life, he would make himself forget that he ever loved her.

He finally sat up and swung his legs over the side of the bed. The shanty was quiet, and he wondered if she'd gone into her room and fallen asleep like he had. If that was the case, then he'd talk to her tomorrow. He was hoping that maybe he could make her see that her love for him wasn't real but rather a manifestation of their circumstances.

He got out of the bed and left his room. The door to her room was closed, so he assumed she had, indeed, fallen asleep after all the wild emotions that had been spent.

He went into the living room and sat back in his recliner. For the first time since he'd moved to the swamp, he wished he had a television. He would have loved to turn on some mindless show and lose himself in it. He was so tired of thinking.

Since he didn't have a television, he picked up the book he'd been reading and tried to concentrate on the words on the page. But within minutes he put the book back down. He couldn't focus.

He got out of his chair, deciding he needed a glass of the orange juice that was in his cooler. Immediately, he saw the note on the table.

Needed to talk to somebody. Went to Nola's. Be back later.

With surprise, he went back to her bedroom, wondering if she was already back from Nola's. He opened the door. Her bed was neatly made, and she wasn't there.

He returned to the kitchen, poured himself a glass of juice and sat down at the table. She should be safe at Nola's. Surely if anything had happened to her on the way there, he would have heard about it by now. That was one thing about the swamp: when things happened, the grapevine worked overtime.

In a little while, he'd head out to Nola's so he could make sure Monique got back here safely. He could understand her need to talk to somebody. It didn't surprise him that she wanted to share things with the woman who had been in her life for so long.

He didn't know Nola well, but he knew how much Monique and her sisters all loved her. According to Monique, Nola had been like the favorite aunt who always had candy in her pocket and hugs and kisses for the girls.

She had been Mystique's best friend.

She would have had a key to Mystique's house.

The night of the murder, there had been no forced entry, leaving the police to believe either the front door had been unlocked or the killer had a key.

As far as he knew Nola hadn't even been a suspect in the case. Should she have been? His mind suddenly raced with wild suppositions.

Nola lived in the swamp. It would have been easy for her to eavesdrop at his windows. She could have also easily left the notes for Monique. The woman had a sturdy build and was probably strong as an ox…strong enough to fight with Mystique and slice her throat… strong enough to beat the hell out of Monique. She was a woman who had lived in the swamp alone all her life. She probably owned a gun and would know how to shoot it.

He took a drink of the juice and shook his head. What the hell was he thinking? Why on earth would Mystique's best friend kill her? Apparently, his brain wasn't thinking clearly.

Yet his gut tightened with continued thoughts of Nola. Nola, who had pressed so hard for Pierre Guidry to be arrested for Mystique's murder. Nola, who seemed to know everything that went on in the swamp.

Power and the potential of blackmail. Those were the reasons somebody would want Mystique's client book. Had Nola gone to Mystique's shanty that night with the intent of killing her friend and taking the book?

Had Monique run to the arms of her mother's killer for comfort and was she now in danger?

He jumped up out of his chair and hurried to his bedroom where he put on his holster and gun.

Adrenaline suddenly pumped through his veins as a sense of urgency filled him. If he was wrong about this, then no harm, no foul. However, if his gut was right, then Monique could be in mortal danger.

He left his shanty, his heart beating frantically in his chest. He ran through the swamp, fear for her a living, breathing entity inside him.

How long had she been gone? Dammit, how long had he slept? Was he wrong about all this? Would he find Monique and Nola peacefully seated on Nola's sofa and having a chat? Or was he already too late? Had Nola already killed Monique and dragged her body out into the swamp to be discovered later?

He ran like he'd never run before, unmindful of the branches that tried to snag him, swiping at the Spanish moss that threatened to blind him. Finally, Nola's shanty came into view. He raced to the front door and instead of knocking, he tried to open it. It was locked.

"Nola!" he yelled and banged on the door.

"Jacque!" Monique screamed from inside and the terror in that scream gave him a strength he didn't know he possessed.

He crashed his shoulder into the door. Once…twice… and it sprang open. With a deep breath he stepped inside.

Instantly he saw Monique. She rose from the floor by the end of the sofa, blood coming from wounds in her arms and on her chest.

"Behind you," she screamed.

At that moment Nola jumped on his back, and a sharp pain nearly stole his breath away. He knew she'd stabbed him. Still, he managed to yank the woman off him, and he cast her to the floor.

She held a big bloody knife in her hand, and she stood from the floor with a guttural cry. She came at him again and stabbed out, but he kicked her in her stomach, and she fell backward.

His breaths came in labored pants as he pulled his gun. "Nola, stop, or I'll shoot you," he said. He didn't even want to look at Monique, for if he gazed at her all bloody and afraid, he knew without question he would shoot Nola dead. "Drop the knife, Nola. It's over."

"She attacked me for no reason," Nola exclaimed. "She came at me like a vicious animal. I had to protect myself from her." She dropped her knife, and he kicked it to the side out of her reach. "I'm sorry, I… I didn't mean to go after you, but I'm scared and…"

"Shut up," Jacque snapped. "Monique, are you all right?" he asked without taking his eyes off Nola.

"I… I'm okay." Her voice still radiated tremendous fear, and she had begun to quietly weep. "Sh-she killed my mother, Jacque. She's the one who beat me and tried to kill me, too."

"That's utterly ridiculous," Nola scoffed. "Can't you see her grief has obviously muddied her brain?"

"I told you to shut up," Jacque said. "Monique, honey, do you have your phone?" In his peripheral vision, he saw her move to the sofa and grab her purse. "Call Daniel. Tell him to hurry before I kill Nola."

"I'm an innocent woman," Nola cried. "I didn't do anything but try to protect myself."

Jacque kept his gun pointed at her while Monique made the call. The wound in his back burned, and chest pain radiated out to his shoulder, making it difficult for him to draw a deep breath. However, he wasn't concerned about himself. He was worried about Monique. How many times had Nola stabbed or cut her?

After she made the call to the police, she collapsed, still weeping softly, in a chair by the sofa while he held Nola captive on the floor.

Monique's eyes were now closed, and she'd gone silent, making Jacque's worry about her rise higher. "Monique… you with me?" he asked.

Her eyes fluttered open. "I'm here." She closed her eyes once again.

Thankfully, it wasn't long before he heard the sounds of sirens in the distance. And it wasn't long after that when Daniel and four of his men came into the shanty.

Daniel took one look at the scene and then gazed at Jacque. "Somebody want to tell me what's going on here?" he asked.

"Nola killed my mother," Monique said as more tears once again filled her eyes. "She has Mama's client book. It's in the kitchen with her cookbooks. She confessed everything to me. She was going to blackmail the clients, but my mother refused to do that, so Nola killed her."

"Jacque, put your gun away," Daniel said. He reached down and yanked Nola to her feet.

Jacque put his gun back into his holster as Daniel handcuffed Nola.

"They have it all wrong," Nola said desperately to anyone who might listen to her. "Monique has gone crazy. I would never harm a hair on Mystique's head. I would never…"

"Shut up, Nola," Jacque said once again. "We need an ambulance for Monique," he said urgently to Daniel. "As you can see, she's been hurt."

"EMTs are coming," Daniel replied. He turned and looked at Luke Madison, one of the officers who had come in with him. "Get Nola out of here," he said. "Get her into a jail cell, and we'll sort all this out later."

By the time Nola was escorted out, the EMTs came in with a stretcher. It was only when Monique was carried out that Jacque felt a sense of relief.

"Johnny… Roger, keep this shanty locked down and under guard until I sort things out at the station," Daniel instructed. "And get that client book into an evidence bag. Before you do that, make sure you take plenty of photographs showing where it's located." He turned back to Jacque. "Needless to say, I need you to come into the station so I can get a full picture of what happened here."

"No problem," Jacque replied. He turned to head out the door, hoping he had enough breath to walk to his car and drive into town.

"Dammit, Jacque, your whole back is bloody," Daniel said in alarm.

"Yeah, Nola managed to stab me before I got her under

control. I think she might have nicked my lung because I'm having a bit of trouble breathing," he admitted.

Daniel released another string of curses. "The ambulance has already left. Can you make it to my car? I'll drive you to the hospital."

Minutes later, in the passenger seat of Daniel's car, Jacque leaned his head back and closed his eyes.

It was over. It was finally all over. The killer had been identified and arrested, and Monique was no longer in any danger. It would be safe now for her to go back to her shanty, back to her own life. And he would return to his own life. It was what was best for both of them.

Eventually she would forget that she'd thought herself in love with him. She would find a man who could love her without reservation, and he'd go back to his life as a loner.

He just didn't know why these thoughts made it even more difficult for him to breathe.

Chapter Thirteen

Monique was taken directly into the emergency room where Dr. Harmon treated her for her wounds. She received eight stitches for a slice in her arm, although no stitches were required for the wound on her chest which had just been a glancing swipe of the knife. Dr. Harmon was confident it would heal up nicely on its own.

What wouldn't heal up for a very long time to come was the utter devastation of Nola's betrayal and her killing Mystique. Monique couldn't even begin to understand that kind of evil, and it made her sick to think about.

"I think that does it," Dr. Harmon said as he finished bandaging the chest wound. "Keep antibiotic cream on it and keep it covered for the next couple of days. If it gets red or looks like it's getting infected, come back in to see me immediately."

"I will and thank you, Dr. Harmon," she replied.

"I believe your sisters are out in the waiting room," he said.

"What about Jacque? Jacque LeBlanc. Do you know if he is in the waiting room, too?" she asked.

"Actually, he's being treated right now by Dr. Berman for a stab wound and a collapsed lung," Dr. Harmon replied.

"What?" Horror swept through her. Jacque had been hurt? He'd been stabbed and now had a collapsed lung? A sob burst out of her, a sob followed by another and another as she thought of the man who had saved her life so many times before…the man she loved with all her heart.

"Here…here, dear." Dr. Harmon awkwardly patted her on her back. "From everything I've heard, he's going to be just fine. Although I imagine he'll be staying here with us for a night or two."

"Can I see him later?" she asked and swiped away her tears.

"I doubt if he'll be allowed any visitors this evening. Monique, from what I've heard, you've just been through quite a traumatic time. What you need to do now is go home and get some rest. I'm sure you'll be able to visit Mr. LeBlanc sometime tomorrow."

She nodded, and minutes later she walked out of the emergency room and into the waiting, loving arms of her sisters. Both of them hugged her with tender care, and then Angelique led the way to her car in the parking lot. Dominique got into the back, and Monique got into the passenger seat.

Night had fallen, but the moon was a big round lighted ball in the sky that spilled down beautiful silvery light. Stars shone brilliantly from the dark canvas of the sky.

"Monique, why don't you come spend the night with me and Daniel?" Angelique suggested as she started up her car. "You know we have a nice guest bedroom."

"Thanks, sis, but I'd really rather go back to Jacque's

for the night," Monique replied. "Most of my things are there, and I'll be more comfortable there for the night."

She hoped Jacque hadn't locked up his house when he'd gone to Nola's. If that was the case, then she'd just head back to her own shanty. She would be safe now to walk around without fear.

The conversation quickly moved on to Nola. "I hope she goes away until hell freezes over," Dominique said after Monique told them about her final moments with the woman.

"She'll probably be in jail for the rest of her life," Angelique replied.

"Not only will she be facing murder charges, but she'll also face attempted murder charges for trying to kill me," Monique replied.

Even though the topic of conversation was the killer, Monique was nearly consumed with her worry for Jacque. However, there was nothing she could do about that for the night. At least he was at the hospital where he belonged.

"I never suspected her," Dominique said. "I would have never believed Nola was the killer."

"Nobody suspected her," Angelique replied.

"I always believed it was a man who killed her," Monique said.

"Yeah, me, too," Dominique replied.

"I can't believe how strong and brave you've been through all this," Angelique said with a glance at Monique. "I guess this means the baby of the family has truly grown up."

Monique released a small laugh. "I have, indeed."

They continued to talk about the case and their utter

sense of betrayal until they reached the swamp. "At least we have the closure that we all needed," Dominique said as Angelique parked the car.

"While the outcome has been tragic for us, we now have the answers we all needed. We can finally move on with our lives without this shadow hanging over us," Angelique said.

"And we have each other," Dominique said.

"And that's a great thing," Monique replied, eternally grateful for her older sisters' love and support.

"Monique, want us to walk you in?" Dominque asked once Angelique pulled up at the swamp entrance.

"No, I'll be fine," she assured them as she opened her car door. "The moon is full, the killer is in jail, and I don't have to be afraid anymore. I'll just talk to you both sometime tomorrow."

Minutes later Monique followed the trail to Jacque's place. It was all finally over. She didn't have to look over her shoulder or clutch a knife or be afraid as she walked the path.

While she was happy Nola was in jail where she belonged, how could she happy with Jacque in the hospital? How could she be thrilled that it would now be time for her to pack up her things and leave his shanty? Yes, her mother's murder had been solved, but there was still so much worry, so much heartache left.

She finally reached his shanty and was grateful to find the front door unlocked. She went inside and immediately lit several of the lanterns that were placed around the living room.

She sank down on the sofa and looked over at the empty recliner. A collapsed lung... Worry for him squeezed her chest tight. Hopefully the doctor would fix it with no complications, and Jacque would be back here where he belonged tomorrow.

Then it would be time for her to go back where he thought *she* belonged. More than anything she'd wanted him to tell her he loved her. She'd wanted to make her home here with him. But that hadn't happened. It wasn't going to happen, so tomorrow it would be time to pack up her things and move back to her shanty.

Tears burned her eyes. There had been so much emotion in the day. First had been the heartbreak of learning about the loss of his wife and child, followed by the anguish of him telling her he didn't love her. Then there had been the terror of believing that Nola was going to kill her and now the worry about Jacque.

The fight with Nola had felt like it had gone on forever. She'd had to dodge and weave to keep Nola's knife from making a killing stab. She had thrown things at the woman and had jumped over furniture to keep Nola at bay.

It was no wonder she was suddenly completely exhausted. What she now needed more than anything was to go to bed. Besides, she wanted to be up and at the hospital early the next morning to check on Jacque.

With a weary sigh, she got up from the sofa and turned off all the lanterns except one. She started to carry it with her to her bedroom, but then paused in the open doorway of Jacque's room.

She really wanted to be in his bed where his scent would surround her and sweet memories would send her off to sleep. Surely, he wouldn't mind since he wasn't here.

She went into her room and changed out of the jeans

and green shirt she'd worn and into her pale pink night-shirt. Returning to his bedroom, she sat on the edge of his bed.

On impulse, even knowing she was snooping, she opened the top drawer of his nightstand. She released a small gasp as she saw the framed photo inside. With gentle care, she picked it up and stared at the two people Jacque had loved and lost.

Lauren had been a beautiful blonde with bright blue eyes and little Lily had looked just like her mother. They both were laughing, and even though Monique didn't know the two, her heart squeezed tight with grief.

It was the sadness over two innocent people who had died needlessly and the sorrow that their deaths had brought that had forever changed the man who had loved them.

She put the photo back in the drawer and then got in beneath the sheets that smelled of Jacque. Even though he professed not to love Monique, would he ever seek love again? She doubted it.

She knew that once she left here, he would go back to being a loner, not inviting anyone to get close to him. He would once again shut himself off from laughter and any semblance of happiness. That broke her heart almost as much as him not loving her.

Bullfrogs croaked, creating a familiar lullaby that soothed her. She must have fallen asleep, for when she opened her eyes again, the sun was just breaking over the horizon. She got out of the bed and made it, then left his bedroom and went into her own.

She changed out of her nightgown and into her terry robe. More than anything she wanted a shower. She'd have to be careful to keep her bandages dry, but she felt the need to clean herself from yesterday's trauma. And she wanted to wash away Nola's touch.

It was still difficult to believe that Nola had killed her mother all for the love of money. She'd slashed Mystique's throat. How did a woman do such a thing to another woman who had been her friend for years? Monique would never understand that kind of evil.

With these kinds of disturbing thoughts plaguing her mind, she started the shower and then got in. The shower made her feel a little better, but not much because once she was dressed again, she began the task of packing up her things.

Tears burned at her eyes with each item of clothing she folded and put in her bag. It was going to take more than a single trip to get everything back to her shanty. Maybe she'd call her sisters later and see if one of them could help her.

She wanted it all moved out while Jacque was gone. It would be easier that way. No emotional goodbyes, no tears shed on her part… Just a clean break with what might have been.

While she worked, she kept an eye on the time. As soon as it was late enough, she did want to go to the hospital to check on him. There was no question she was worried about him. Hopefully the doctor had been able to take care of him, and he'd be just fine.

He'd saved her life yesterday, and in the process, Nola had stabbed him in the back, deep enough to hit his lung. As he'd held Nola under gunpoint, he'd shown no sign of the tremendous pain he must have been in. He'd shown nothing but strength and command of the situation, and Monique knew he had done that for her.

It was a few minutes before nine when she checked in at the hospital to see what room Jacque was in. Once she had the information, she hurried down the hallway. The scents of coffee and bacon lingered in the air, letting her know that breakfast had either just finished or was still being delivered to patient rooms.

When she reached room 107, she stepped inside, and her heart expanded at the sight of him. He was sitting up in the bed, a breakfast tray across his lap. The blue-flowered hospital gown did nothing to detract from his attractiveness. When he saw her, a wide smile curved his lips.

"Jacque." She whispered his name as tears blurred her vision. She stepped up to the side of his bed and, unable to help herself, she took hold of his hand and squeezed it. "You look okay. Are you really okay?"

"I'm fine… Don't cry, Monique. I'm good, and I should come home later this afternoon or first thing tomorrow."

She released his hand and pulled up a nearby chair and sat at his side. "I heard you were stabbed and had a collapsed lung. I didn't know, Jacque. I didn't even know she had stabbed you."

"The good thing is the nick to my lung wasn't too bad, and the doctor fixed me right up. I was on oxygen all night, but they pulled me off that early this morning. How are you? The last time I saw you, you were pretty bloody."

"I'm okay. I have a few stitches in my arm, and she slashed me across my chest, but that didn't even need stitches."

He smiled at her again. "You solved the case, Monique. You solved it just like you wanted to."

A small laugh escaped her. "Not by my brain power. It was just sheer chance that I saw my mother's book in her kitchen."

"At least the crime has finally been solved."

"And I'm no longer in danger," she replied. "In fact, I'm packing up my things today and heading back to my shanty since you no longer need to babysit me." She kept her tone light despite the intense pain that wrenched her heart.

"There was certainly no rush for you to leave, but I'm sure you're eager to get back to your real life," he replied. "Now you can live your life freely and not be afraid anymore."

She'd hoped to spend her life with him, loving him and him loving her, but that wasn't going to happen. She pushed her chair back and stood, needing to escape before she burst into more tears. "Well, I just wanted to check in on you," she said. "I'm glad you're doing okay, Jacque. As you know, I'll always be eternally grateful to you for everything you've done for me."

"It was my pleasure, Monique," he replied softly. "And now I hope you have a wonderful life."

She said a quick goodbye and then escaped the room. She didn't begin to weep until she was in her car driving back to the swamp. Only then did her tears fall because the man she loved with all her heart and soul didn't love her back.

It had been seven days since Monique had packed up and left Jacque's shanty. Life returned to normal. She'd thrown herself into her job, working long hours to keep her busy. She had a pleasant lunch with her sisters, but all the while her heart ached with an unrelenting pain.

She'd heard that Jacque had returned home from the hospital, but in the seven days that had passed, she didn't see or hear from him. It was as if their time together had never really happened. Except it had, and the end result was that she still felt gutted by it all.

The town buzzed with the news that Nola had killed the voodoo queen. She remained in jail awaiting trial. While Monique didn't like the way district attorney Jackson Scott conducted his personal life, she knew he was a good attorney who would see to it that Nola got the maximum punishment for her crimes.

On Monday, Monique worked from nine until five, and when she left work, she was particularly tired. She hadn't been sleeping well but was hoping tonight she would get some good rest.

When she got home, she changed from her work clothes into a red sundress she often wore in the evenings. It was comfortable and cool, as the last several days had been particularly warm with little breeze. Once she'd changed, she made herself a salad for dinner, but only picked at it with little appetite.

Somehow, she knew she needed to pull herself together. Somehow, she needed to forget how much she loved Jacque. But she didn't know how to do that. Thoughts of him invaded her mind a million times a day, and dreams of him haunted what little sleep she got.

She finally tossed the last of her salad into the trash and then curled up on the sofa with several lanterns lit near her. For the past seven nights, she had read until bedtime. It helped pass the long, lonely evenings that had once been filled with conversation and laughter.

She'd only been reading for about a half an hour when a knock fell on her door. With a frown, wondering who it could be, she got up to answer it.

Jacque. He stood on her front porch with evening shadows darkening his face. "Hi, Monique. Mind if I come in for a minute?"

"Of course not." Her heartbeat triple-timed in her chest as she opened the door wider to allow him entry. She drank in his features as the lanterns lit them and breathed in his achingly familiar scent. Why was he here? Had something come up in the case against Nola? If that was the case, then surely Daniel would be here.

"Uh…would you like something to drink?" she asked as he sat gingerly on her sofa.

"No, thanks, I'm good," he replied.

"How are you feeling?" She sat a little distance away from him on the sofa. Still, she was close enough to breathe in the scent of him. Despite everything that had happened, it smelled like home.

"I'm fine…no worse for wear," he replied. "What about you?"

"I'm fine, too."

For a moment, an awkward silence fell between them. "Was there something…?" she began.

"Yes…there's something," he said quickly. His green eyes stared into hers. "You've absolutely ruined me."

She looked at him in surprise. "What do you mean?"

"I was perfectly satisfied living my miserable life, and then you came along. You forced me to smile, and you made me laugh. You reminded me how to have a real conversation and look forward to getting up in the mornings." He leaned toward her. "Monique, you ruined me by loving me despite my scowls and attempts to distance myself from you."

With each word he said, a fragile hope began to well up in her heart. But she remained silent, needing to hear more from him…so much more.

"Since you left my shanty, nothing has been right. I eat breakfast, and I miss you sitting across from me at my table. I go out to fish, and I miss having you on the bank next to me. The evenings seem to go on forever… long, torturous hours of utter silence."

Even though she couldn't remember the last time he'd talked so much, he still hadn't said what she wanted most to hear. "Why are you here, Jacque?" she finally asked.

His green eyes filled with a warmth of emotion that threatened to steal her breath from her. "I've come to get you and take you back to my shanty where you belong. Monique, I'm madly, wildly in love with you, and I need you in my life forever."

There were the words she'd wanted most to hear from him. "Say it again," she whispered softly.

He stood and pulled her up and into his arms. "I love you, Monique. I can't imagine my life without you. You're the little woman who has stolen my heart. Will you come live with me and be my wife?"

"Yes, oh yes." She barely got the words out of her mouth when his lips took hers in a tender kiss that spoke eloquently of his love for her.

As the kiss continued, tears filled her eyes…happy tears because she knew she was going to have a wonderful life with him.

When the kiss ended, he looked deep into her eyes. "I want to marry you and build a family with you," he said. "Fate is giving me a second chance at happiness, and I'm not going to be the loner of the swamp any longer."

She knew he would always hold Lauren and Lily deep in his heart, but there was more than enough room there for her. "And I'm going to make you smile at least ten times a day," she said.

He laughed. "Honey, with you in my life, smiling is going to be easy."

He kissed her again, and as she tasted his desire, his love for her, she knew with certainty she was going to be right where she belonged…with Jacque.

* * * * *

[illegible]
[illegible]
[illegible]
[illegible]
[illegible]
[illegible]
[illegible]
[illegible]

[illegible]
[illegible]
[illegible]
[illegible]

Get up to 4 Free Books!

We'll send you 2 free books from each series you try
PLUS a free Mystery Gift.

Both the **Harlequin Intrigue**® and **Harlequin**® **Romantic Suspense** series feature compelling novels filled with heart-racing action-packed romance that will keep you on the edge of your seat.

YES! Please send me 2 FREE novels from the Harlequin Intrigue or Harlequin Romantic Suspense series and my FREE gift (gift is worth about $10 retail). I may cancel anytime by emailing ReaderServiceInfo@Harlequin.com or by calling 1-800-873-8635. If I don't cancel, I will receive 6 brand-new Harlequin Intrigue Larger-Print books every month and be billed just $7.19 each in the U.S. or $7.99 each in Canada, or 4 brand-new Harlequin Romantic Suspense books every month and be billed just $6.39 each in the U.S. or $7.19 each in Canada, a savings of 20% off the cover price. It's quite a bargain! Shipping and handling is just 75¢ per book in the U.S. and $1.75 per book in Canada.* I understand that accepting the free books and gift places me under no obligation to buy anything—they are mine to keep for free no matter what I decide.

Choose one:
☐ **Harlequin Intrigue Larger-Print**
(199/399 BPA G3CD)

☐ **Harlequin Romantic Suspense**
(240/340 BPA G3CD)

☐ **Or Try Both!**
(199/399 & 240/340 BPA G3CE)

Name (please print)

Address ___ Apt. #

City ___ State/Province ___ Zip/Postal Code

Email: Please check this box ☐ if you would like to receive newsletters and promotional emails from Harlequin Enterprises ULC and its affiliates. You can unsubscribe anytime.

Mail to the **Harlequin Reader Service:**
IN U.S.A.: P.O. Box 1341, Buffalo, NY 14240-8531
IN CANADA: P.O. Box 603, Fort Erie, Ontario L2A 5X3

Want to explore our other series or interested in ebooks? Visit www.ReaderService.com or call 1-800-873-8635.

HIHRS2603